D1043555

UNBREAK MY HEART

Triumph Series Book I

KASHINDA T. MARCHE

Middleton Public Library
7425 Hubbard Ave
Middleton, WI 53562

Copyright 2019 © Kashinda T. Marche

All rights reserved. No part of this book may be reproduced in any form or by any electronic or mechanical means, including information storage and retrieval systems, without permission in writing from the publisher, except by reviewers, who may quote brief passages in a review.

ISBN: 978-1-943179-50-3

Library of Congress: 2019900661

Published by Imperial Publishing House, a subsidiary of Nayberry Publications, Opelika, AL.

For copyright issues, including permissions for use or to report improper use, contact Shani Dowdell, 334-787-0733.

FOLLOW US ONLINE

ACKNOWLEDGEMENTS

First and foremost, I would like to acknowledge an awesome God for making all things possible in my life.

A very special thanks to my daughter, Asia, for encouraging me to pursue my own journey of self-discovery. You motivated me to put this project in motion.

Thank you to my step-dad, Keith, for always looking out for me.

I appreciate Danielle aka Kisha for being my best friend for over twenty five years.

I feel blessed to have my Godmother Idell in my life. I thank you for being such a wonderful influence and a kind spirit who has never let me down.

Kashinda

DEDICATION

This book is dedicated to my mother, Elaine and my daughter Asia E. Marche.

Also, to my younger siblings Samad & Ebony and the rest of my extended family & friends who have inspired me in many ways.

It is my hope that you can receive and use this story as a tool of encouragement reminding you to declare victory in your lives.

To all those who may be battling or affected by any form of chronic illness, know that you are not alone through the struggle.

I love you all from the bottom of my heart.

Peace and blessings to us all.

CHAPTER ONE
THE BEGINNING OF IT ALL

The gray clouds clustered above us. It was pouring down raining and had a chill to it. Trish and I were the only fools out walking the block. Huddled together under the crappy umbrella we shared, the blustering wind blew so hard that it flipped the damn thing upward.

We laughed.

"This is crazy," we said simultaneously.

"Oh snap!" I shouted when a car sped by and splashed Trish. I felt bad for her. She was the one closest to the curb, and she got drenched by a puddle of dirty water. She was furious. Her new denim shorts were now spotted with mud.

Trish hollered out, "You jerk!" and threw up her middle finger.

The driver couldn't have heard her. We stood there for a moment and watched as the rear lights of the car became bright red, before turning the corner. We continued to walk, but Trish made sure she was on the other side of me.

"Stupid ass," Trish mumbled.

"For real tho'," I muttered.

We were shocked to see the black car had circled the block and slowly pulled up alongside me as if I were the one who shouted out at him. When I saw a guy crack his window, I rushed to say to him, "It wasn't me who yelled, but you did splatter my girl with that damn water in the street. You need to slow down before you hurt somebody."

Trish leaned forward to look inside the car. Still angry, she said, "Dag, you ugly. Just keep going about your business, yo'."

I chuckled and kneeled beside Trish to gain a better view of him. I heard him laugh also. Shaking my head, I asked, "Why are you laughing? She just called you ugly."

He was an older man, dressed in a dirty uniform like he had just gotten off work. He replied, "She funny, right?" The fumes that escaped from his opened window made my nose twinge.

I scrunched my face. "Yup, but you not."

During this exchange, the rain stopped. Trish nudged me as if hinting at something. She tried to convince me to ask him for a ride home. When I stood back up and turned to look at her, he pulled off. Without any hesitation, I boldly answered, "Hell no, did you see him?"

She said, "Yea, girl, that's why I was telling you to go for it."

Sarcastically, I replied, "Ha-ha-ha, you mad funny. Now, I'm out. I'm going in the house and so should you."

Trish agreed as she handed me what was left of my umbrella. "Here, take this piece of shit with you."

We then proceeded to go our separate ways.

As I walked home, I heard someone yell out to me with a heavy accent, "You want a ride?" I curiously looked over, and it was that man again. He came back.

I didn't give my answer much thought. I quickly responded, "Yes, and you betta not try anything stupid." I hopped in.

He chuckled at me and said, "No, I never would do that."

I was anxious as hell but continued to try to make small talk so that he wouldn't notice my youth or my nervousness. I couldn't avoid rambling, not giving him a chance to answer. "Where you from? What kind of work you do that got you so dirty?"

After a moment of silence, finally, he said, "I'm Haitian." He also told me he was a car doctor, and I interpreted that to mean an auto mechanic.

7

"Okaaaay," I said. I didn't bother pressing that topic any further. I was already able to tell how poor his English was. Besides that, his car smelled too much like motor oil.

I was careful not to show this guy exactly where I lived. Instead, I had him drop me off at the corner of Grove Street and 18th Ave. I thanked him, and that was it. I walked the rest of the way home, which was only a couple of houses from the corner.

About a week later, I was walking down Grove Street again to meet up with my crew, and as I crossed the street, I saw a familiar car ride past me. It was a black Nissan Maxima™. Sure enough, it was the dude from the rainy day. We never did get each other's names when he dropped me off, so I was caught off guard when he honked at me. He pulled his car over, and for some strange reason, it brought a smile to my face. This time, I got in his car as if I had known him for a long time.

My teen years began in the streets of Irvington, New Jersey, in the late 80s. It was rough back then, but I had my fun times too. It wasn't until later that I realized those days were the beginning of my life. I learned one lesson after another.

During the summers, my friends and I would hang out on the steps of our front porches, playing Double Dutch jump rope. We heard music coming from the drug dealers' cars so loud you could literally feel the vibration as they rode by. Naughty By Nature's "O.P.P."© played through the speakers with a high level of bass making our heads turn and causing us to sing along. We gave shout-outs to the drivers. The owners of the neighborhood bodegas, with lust in their eyes, would say to us young girls from around the way, "Aye Mami, lookin' good," as we bought loosie cigarettes and five cent candy. My hood reeked of all the disadvantages any kid would need to make lots of stupid choices.

On a typical, dry Saturday afternoon I waited on the steps of an abandoned house in the area, and my girls showed up soon after because this was our daily meeting place. We would figure out what we'd be getting into for the day. We enjoyed drinking beer in Vailsburg Park. Alcohol was always a part of the plan. Particularly, our signature brand was that of a black-labeled bottle with an image depicting an island far away. We liked St. Ides™ beer. We drank because it allowed us to mentally escape our realities. It gave us an excuse to enjoy impulsive behaviors. Lots of Doublemint™ gum and baby lotion assisted in masking the scent of alcohol from our parents.

We were loud and free when we got buzzed. *Maybe too free.* There was one instance where we thought we had done too much. One of our regular Saturdays in the park. It was after 11 p.m.

"Hey, what are you girls out here doing this time of night?" a white female police officer shouted out, scaring the shit out of us. We hauled ass towards home base—the meeting porch. I sometimes wondered if our parents were so distracted with their own lives that they did not notice how drunk their teenage daughters really were.

My crew was made of my two best friends: Monica aka "Tyson" was the reserved one of the group who owned every color Champion™ t-shirt made. Her hair was thick with tight curls and the complexion of honey. Very smart, but always afraid of getting busted by her mom, and Tyson's mom was a true pistol, ready to bust someone's ass at any moment. Tyson had confided in us that her mom was physically abusive toward her stepfather. An ordinary day in their house involved Tyson overhearing her mom throwing around infidelity accusations and disrespectful gestures, which made Tyson see men as weak and easily controllable. We gave her the name Tyson because of her mom's behavior.

However, Trish was actually the feisty one. Short and curvaceous. Her weekly new high-topped sneakers meant everything to her. She wore them with pride and still was down to jack a chick up in a heartbeat. Trish's mother was well known in the neighborhood for selling crack. They moved into the house of one of our hood's most successful drug dealers. We asked if they were also being tricked out by him, but Trish never admitted to it. Trish would always say as she bit her nails, "A dude betta have enough money to take care of me and my kids." We laughed at her because motherhood wasn't exactly what we saw when we looked at Trish, but she wasn't joking.

Then, there's me. Tharisse—tall, thin, ponytail to the back. A jeans and t-shirt kinda girl. I lacked any curves, unlike Trish, so I hid in baggy jeans which also kept me from being teased about wearing high waters.

I was considered the mature one; the girl that knew a little about a lot. I had older cousins that I was very close to, and they taught me lots of stuff. It was only right that I shared those teachings with my girls.

Ironically, we all lived in households under the rule of a stepfather, and none of us were particularly fond of these so-called men but knew we had to respect them because our moms were with them. I had known my real dad before he died when I was about nine-years-old or so. So, our stepfathers were practically strangers to us. Our views of men weren't given a fair chance. *Were we doomed?*

11

There had to be someone we could trust to get our drinks, so I would always suggest that Trish be responsible for the liquor store run. She knew someone much older than us who was actually willing to cop our drinks. Our secret was safe with her as long as we could buy her a beer too. Managing to scrounge up enough change was a challenge for all of us, but somehow, we pulled it off.

"Trish, go tell your girl we need a store run," is what I'd say to her, to which Trish would respond, "Why I always gotta be the one?"

Tyson would then suck her teeth. "You act like we know somebody who can get it for us, Trish. Stop acting dumb."

I would become an instant mediator even as I laughed at Tyson; she was ready to lay one on Trish. "Y'all huzzies need to cut it out, and let's just get the damn drinks and chill out. Damn, y'all both acting dumb."

I wasn't sure if they'd listen to me anyway, but it usually worked. We would get our beer from Trish's friend and head to the park. By the time the sun went down, we were coming around the corner, and there they were, the boys from our neighborhood, ready to take advantage of us stupidly intoxicated girls in any way they could. But, we weren't easy girls. We played hard to get, especially Tyson; she never gave it up. She'd always say, "Yea, I ain't doing nothing with nobody." Unlike me, she valued her virginity. So, that left me and Trish down for whatever, and Trish loved to fuck.

We'd tease her, "Oh, well, corny ass."

A typical day for us always led to someone getting their reputation tarnished in some way, but we had no idea how our precious teen years were setting the tone for our lives later. My girls and I all seemed to have men issues due to the dynamics of our households.

Chilling in the park, getting tipsy, joking around, telling our stories of what life should be like, as if any of us really had a clue, was how we spent most of our days. We became sisters to one another even though we had biological siblings. We considered ourselves "street" sisters and had even created a name for our clique, which we got from the beer we loved to drink. It made us identifiable on the block.

At the time, we didn't think we should have been more aware of how building each other's confidence and self-esteem would have been beneficial. We didn't tell each other we loved one another. It wasn't something we considered important. Although, I believed when my girls were alone in their own homes, they all thirsted for that kind of assurance.

13

Aside from my peer commitments, I had my own demons trying to invade me, and I had to find ways to cope with my perplexing household drama. I had confessed to my crew that one day, when I was sweeping the kitchen floor, my parents' bedroom door wasn't closed all the way. As I peeked in, I saw my stepfather crushing something. Then, he and my mom sniffed it in their noses using what looked like a little straw. "What the hell is up with that? Do y'all think he was gettin' her high?" I knew my mom seemed agitated most of the time. Could it have had anything to do with what my stepfather gave her?

Trish was the first to say, "T, you not stupid. You know what the hell they were doing."

Tyson said, "Well, I don't know about none of that, so girl, I don't know." She just shook her head.

I was embarrassed at first but then thought we all had jacked up issues going on. Besides, they were my peeps. I should be able to let them in on something so bothersome to me. Quite naturally, from the first time I saw such a thing taking place, it made me curious to find out what was going on. I'd pay close attention to my mom and stepdad's behavior, but nothing was unusual about that either. There were times when my parents left out of the house, where I'd look for that stuff. I never found anything, so I thought maybe it was a one-time thing.

14

But nah, I caught them in the act again. They were definitely getting high, and I lost all respect. I knew from watching TV drugs weren't cool. Although doing them seemed to be the thing to get into during those times, I decided the drug life wasn't for me. That was one decent choice I made.

Cliff, my stepfather, worked every day and was his typical annoying self. I'd often hear him reinforcing his position. "I have the right to do as I damn well please as long as I'm busting my ass bringing in the income," he would assert, and my mom always begged to differ.

In spite of all the negative views of men I encountered by that point, I became very sexually familiar with the fellas in the streets. Intimacy was my way of feeding that acceptance factor I so desperately wanted. I loved hard. My teenage mind, still underdeveloped, began to think that a man was the "it" that I needed to be complete as a person, even if I had my reservations. The conflict had begun. Did I want a man to take care of me and hold it against me, or did I want to become independent? Holding my own was a possibility. It was the start of my path to self-destruction.

Unfortunately, I became addicted to the search for love. I found out later that having deep feelings for someone didn't prove to be all I thought it would be.

The more I thought of how life can take us through the bounds of what can seem like hell, the more I ended up thinking back to that rainy day when I got in the car that practically ruined my friend's new outfit.

I finally asked him his name, and he said, "Eugene, and who are you?"

I felt butterflies in the pit of my stomach because I was riding shotgun with a dude.

"Oh me, I'm Tharisse." Eagerly continuing on, I asked, "Why did you beep your horn at me?"

He replied with a big ass grin on his face, "I like what you look like."

Shaking my head in disbelief, I mentally noted that this was not going to go anywhere other than an occasional ride to or from the neighborhood. When he told me he was twenty-three years old, I rolled my eyes at him in disgust.

Was this muthafuka looking for ass? I asked myself.

The negative side of my thinking showed up front and center. I couldn't have been more wrong about what was happening between me and Eugene. It was a feeling down in the crevices of my soul. I didn't know exactly what was to come of us, so I decided to explore. Before I knew it, we were riding around town all the time, grabbing food to eat and talking. We chatted a lot, and although most of the time I barely understood what the hell he was saying, it hadn't occurred to me that something was indeed developing.

As weeks flew by, I realized I'd met the man who became my Mr. Fix-It. Someone who was willing to buy me all the things a sixteen-year-old girl couldn't afford to get for herself. He was the one that bought me jeans from JC Penny™, a store that sold "talls." I never wore another pair of high waters after he started to spoil me. He made sure I had plenty of female toiletries so that I wouldn't run out before my mom could replenish them, and he bought me school supplies. These were needs my parents ignored.

Eugene was even willing to let my friends ride around with us. One Friday evening, Eugene came through the block where my friends and I were chilling on Trish's porch. I damn near jumped off the porch when I saw his car coming up the street.

"Oh, it's like that? Stop playing! Unlock it. Please." I was excited.

"Ah-hah," Trish's little brother said.

"Shut-up." I bent down and looked in the window of Eugene's car. My face spoke a dozen words. It was sticky as hell outside, and I was trying to get in the air conditioning. My expression shook him, and he unlocked the door. I got in quickly. "No uniform tonight? Nice shirt. That's my favorite color," I said as I held my shirt up to the vent.

He was dressed nicely in his navy-blue polo shirt and khaki cargo shorts and smelled of strong cologne. His hair was freshly cut, very low, and sharply shaped up.

"Oh, shit, let me find out you got nice hair!" I ran my hand over his head, on his shoulders, and instantly noticed his head in his shorts misinterpreted my gesture. I ignored that shit. "We going somewhere?" I asked.

He wore a cheesy smile. "It's a surprise."

Not knowing what he had in mind or entertaining the fact that his dick was laying long against his thigh, I asked if he could take all of us to get some White Castle burgers.

He looked at Trish and said, "Sure, let's go."

I had to take a second glance, and luckily for him, his shit had gone down. As we were getting in the car, I turned and looked at Trish. "Why he looked at you like that?" I asked.

Trish just shrugged me off and stated, "Girl, you souped the hell up, and he souped up, too."

We didn't discuss it anymore.

Rob Base's "It Takes Two©" played through the speakers, blasting just like the drug dealers' we'd shout out to. Eugene was looking at us like we were crazy. My girls and I pretended that we were finally somebody as he sped down Lyons Avenue. During the fun, I admit I was a bit on edge. I didn't want us to get into an accident or be pulled over by Irvington Police.

When we all got back to our hood, Eugene gave me a weird look. I told my friends I would join them in a bit. While we were sitting alone in his car, I asked him what was wrong, and he made a statement I did not expect to hear.

"I got money for you."

I didn't know why he would be giving me money, so I cluelessly asked him, "Why would you give me money?"

Eugene said, "'Cause you be my girlfriend."

"Hold up, you mean to tell me if I be your girlfriend you gonna give me money?"

I was hoping he didn't say yes, but he did. There I was sixteen, and I had a boyfriend with a job, a car, and he would give me money, too. I suppose it should've felt odd. Instead, I allowed him to lead me to a grungy motel, and I allowed him to have me. It wasn't like I was a virgin, but after it was over, I felt so dirty. I let the mere thought of being taken care of get the best of me, which of course didn't put a stop to me indulging in that same activity time and time again, paycheck after paycheck. Eugene passed off some serious cash, and my friends enjoyed the ride. They cheered me on like, "Go girl! You gettin' that cash."

As Eugene and I kicked it more and more, he fell in love with me, and eventually I fell in love with him. The idea of giving him all the sex he wanted in exchange for trips to the mall and keeping my pockets full of money didn't appear to me like I was doing anything wrong. There was nothing naïve about me. In my disturbed mind, it was the perfect give-and-take relationship for a young, misunderstood girl who was growing up hating her home life, feeling neglected, and being misguided by her parental role models.

By the time I decided to make our "thing" official, a little over a year had gone by. It was time to expose our relationship to my parents. I finally brought Eugene home to meet the family. My mother, Jackie, was not at all impressed with this man. She found out he was in his twenties, and Jackie's tone and facial expressions when speaking to him made it very clear how she felt about him. When Eugene would greet her, Jackie would reply with silence, a clear sign of annoyance. Eugene dating her seventeen-year-old daughter pissed her off. But, I wasn't a child anymore.

I would come home with new leather coats and new sneakers, and I'd hear from Jackie time and time again, "Don't be bringin' that shit in my house, Tharisse!"

There were occasions when I bought stuff for the whole family, too. Eugene would even bring Cliff bottles of the finest rums and expensive colognes. Cliff would at least respond to Eugene by saying, "Ah shucks. Thanks, man." I suppose that was Eugene's way of bonding with the man of the house.

Despite my mom's disapproval, I continued to see Eugene. Jackie, with her outspoken ways, would always tell me, "Tharisse, there is something that rubs me the wrong way about him, and you shouldn't be running around with someone so much older." But, I figured if he was willing to take care of me by fulfilling my wants and needs, then Jackie should have just let it be.

The relationship I thought was my happily ever after caused more of a strain on the complicated relationship I already had with my mom. I truly just wanted my mommy back, the way it was when I was younger. Instead, we always argued about my comings and goings. Jackie made it perfectly understood that she would never be okay with Eugene, except when he would pass her greeting cards filled with money. It was then that Jackie didn't think Eugene was so bad after all. She would nonchalantly say to him,

"Thank you." There was one thing that Jackie loved a lot, and that was money. It was something I couldn't hold against her, given the fact that I was now being known on the streets as "T-Money." I loved money, too.

It was apparent that Eugene and I had become exclusive given all the time we spent together. At least, that's how it felt. A new season was upon us.

It was a winter morning; Valentine's Day was near. I literally had to drag myself out of bed to head to school. My stomach was queasy, and I felt like I could have slept forever. My mother noticed I wasn't hanging outside as much, but she never really said anything about it. I skipped school that day and decided to chill solo, only because there was a place in Irvington Center that drew my attention. The sign read: Planned Parenthood, and I wanted to go in to see what it was about.

Once I got inside, there was an older white lady with bad posture hunched behind the counter. She had a distracting coffee stain on her white blouse and didn't seem as bothered about it as I was. "Are you in need of counseling?" she asked.

"No, but do you guys do pregnancy testing here?"

She smiled and said, "Yes, dear, we certainly do. Do you believe yourself to be expecting a child?" She sounded both concerned and sarcastic as she handed me a small package.

It was labeled: pregnancy screening. I felt anxious and alone as I peed on a freaking stick. Those next ten minutes felt more like three hours. *Is my life about to change forever?* I wondered while waiting for the results. Once time was up, the counselor checked the results. Without uttering a word, the lady's face loudly spoke volumes. Her face clearly stated, "That's a damn shame!"

My test showed positive. It would be the first of others that followed. The highlighted plus sign hypnotized me as I stared at it. I knew I had to be brave to deal with my mom. So, on that very same day, I went home and chose not to prolong telling my mother I was going to have a baby. I wasn't ready but was smart enough to know I would need her to get through whatever was in store for me.

I called Eugene and told him to come over. He arrived that evening. I asked both him and my mom to come into my room, then I just came out with it.

"Ma, I think I might be pregnant."

She looked directly at Eugene and blurted right back at me, "You think? Tharisse, don't tell me you think you bringing a baby up in here."

Eugene looked at me as he sat fidgeting on the edge of my bed. "Baby?" he asked.

I sat up a little straighter to exude more confidence. "Yea, I took a test earlier today, and it said positive, so… yea, I'm pregnant, Ma."

I noticed the disappointed look on my mother's face. She must have been lost for words because she walked out of my room and slammed the door behind her. Though my emotions were heightened, exhaustion swept over me. The day had drained me. All I wanted at that point was to go to sleep. Perhaps that "knocked-up sleepiness" is an actual thing. Symptom or not, I only hoped tomorrow would be a better day. I told Eugene to go and we'd talk later. He left without expressing any feelings about the announcement I had just made.

All the cozy time spent with Eugene resulted in me being seventeen and pregnant. Jackie didn't like Eugene as it was, and now I was having his baby. Jackie insisted I would regret having a child because I was so young and hadn't finished high school yet, which was ironic because it was the exact age Jackie got pregnant with me. Nonetheless, I was determined to have Eugene's kid.

24

The weeks following finding out I had a little one on the way, my crew and I had quit our normal scene and gone our separate ways, each trying to figure out life the best way we knew how. It felt like something bigger was going on besides us growing apart, but I had no idea that my world as I had come to know it was about to change in a way that would forever impact me.

CHAPTER TWO
DESTINY

For the first five months of my pregnancy, my days and nights were filled with persistent vomiting. I made regular visits to the ER for IV treatment to prevent dehydration. Doctors diagnosed it as a condition called hyperemesis gravidarum, which means excessive vomiting during gestation, and I had a severe case of it, which basically put my unborn child and me at risk. I was even told there was a great chance of the baby not making it to full term because I had lost so much weight and was considered malnourished. This wasn't the news I expected to hear, especially being such a young mother-to-be. But somehow, I wasn't worried. I often leaned on my mother, and she said things like, "Tharisse, you sure got yourself in some shit, now didn't you?"

I'd reply in a weak voice, "Ma, please don't trip. I'm already messed up, and I'm sorry."

She would shake her head at me. She gave me looks that pierced right through me. Even though Jackie made me feel some type of way, I felt in my heart that my little one was going to bless the world with its presence.

Now what was interesting is how Eugene's presence made me just as sick as carrying the baby. I couldn't stand to be around him, and when he would dress up and drench himself in that awful cologne, I'd practically throw up on him. I cursed him out on a regular basis, saying things like, "Why are you here? Get the hell away from me! Don't look at me!"

Eugene didn't let my words keep him away. Eugene's reaction wasn't exactly screaming excitement when it came to having his first child, but he did his best, making sure I had what I needed while keeping enough distance to avoid wearing my vomit. I don't know why I treated him so badly while I carried his baby. Maybe it was a hormonal thing because it wasn't like I hated him for getting me pregnant.

As the months passed on, I was finally feeling a little better. I stopped throwing up just in time to celebrate my eighteenth birthday. Jackie and Cliff took me out for dinner to one of my favorite places: Red Lobster. I was appreciative, but it was not enough to convince me that they accepted the situation I had placed my family in.

While I ate my crab legs, I snuck a peek at everyone. I wasn't surprised by the gloominess they each wore on their faces. Being the person I am, I tried to perk up the mood just enough to get through the evening.

I asked my younger siblings, "You guys excited to be having a niece or nephew?"

My little brother, Junior, said, "T, you gonna let me play my video game with your baby?"

I told him, "Of course you can play with the baby, Junior."

Food still in his mouth, he mumbled, "Okay."

My little sister didn't say anything, as usual.

I jokingly asked Cliff, "You ready for another child in the house, *Grandpa?*"

He just shrugged his shoulders and said to Jackie, "I guess we don't have a choice, do we, hun?"

I was the one who asked the question, but he replied to my mother. They always played those little games when it came to me needing something as if it required some thought process. The mood at dinner was a bust, so I just tried to enjoy my meal.

When we arrived back home, I gave a dry, "Thanks for dinner," and went to my room.

I started to feel the life growing inside of me and knew everything was going to be alright. My unborn child was beginning to move around, and I took it as my baby's way of communicating to me that we were going to be okay.

The positive progression of the gestation didn't take away the hatred I was feeling underneath.

The pregnancy was doing a number on my physical appearance. I was already battling low self-esteem, so imagine how I felt when I looked in the mirror and saw a face that had the biggest nose and skin that had darkened at least three shades. My voice had gotten even deeper in tone, which led me to believe I was having a boy. I thought I looked and sounded like a man. I felt so unpretty. Some of the changes I went through I assumed to be normal, according to the books I had been reading in preparation for becoming a new mother. I tried so hard to bond with the life inside of me but couldn't get past all the agony.

Before long, the visits to the prenatal clinic were getting scheduled closer together. The doctor, nurses, and specialists were pleased with the fact that my child and I were doing so well. We both had come a long way.

Is this all worth it? I found myself posing this question a lot in my mind. I wanted the baby, but it certainly was a lot of work, not only for me, but for Jackie, my stepfather, and my younger siblings. We were all going through changes because of the fetus I carried. It became a tug of war in my head. I began to think I wasn't as sure as I thought I was. It was becoming more realistic that the duties I had to look forward to were going to be a lot to handle.

I had already missed the latter months of my senior year of high school, which meant I didn't get to enjoy the special moments of prom or graduating with the class of my peers. My street sisters had gotten the word that I was sick during my pregnancy and had reached out with concern. They surprisingly showed up to the baby shower Jackie had put together for the arrival of her first grandchild.

Everything seemed to be on track and going as well as expected, and by the time my due date had approached, the nerves were settling in. I began to pray for what I wanted out of this pregnancy as I assumed new mothers were supposed to do. I prayed for a healthy child—a girl. Yes. I had decided I wanted a beautiful, healthy baby girl that I could connect with, love, and just be the best mother I could be to her.

I ended up going well past my anticipated due date. The doctors determined it would be medically necessary to induce my labor. The baby was maturing and the amniotic fluid was looking a little low, according to the latest ultrasound images. They were getting concerned the baby would begin to ingest the fluid, which can cause pneumonia at birth, and they did not want that to happen.

Having been through so much during my pregnancy, the medical staff sympathized with me, and it was their mission to see to it that I got to hold my newborn after a successful delivery.

A day before my scheduled admittance, I woke out of my sleep with the worse pain in my lower back that I had ever experienced. I felt pressure in my vaginal area. I crawled to my mom's bedside, almost in tears, alerting her that something was going on.

"Ma, I think I need to go in now. It hurts so bad," I cried out to her.

My labor had officially begun naturally, so Jackie got me to the hospital. She pretended to be calm, but I could tell she was just as scared as I was. She darted out the house so fast that she forgot to brush her hair down and still had her nightgown on. She made a call to my aunt that lived right around the corner to come get the kids from the house.

"Tharisse, are you ready for this?" she asked me.

"Yes!" I replied, but I wasn't quite ready for what came next.

During the intense labor, I yelled for it to just be over. I even asked to be shot with a gun to be taken out of my misery. This young mother-to-be wanted to take on childbirth like a trooper and get through the delivery with no drug assistance, but when it became too unbearable, I pleaded with the nurse to give me something to dull the pain.

"Honey, there's no time for that," the nurse sympathetically said to me. "You're going to need to start pushing soon," she added.

I had to endure what felt like torture. Twenty-one hours of excruciating contractions with no epidural. The arctic air hit me as they rolled me into the delivery room. I wouldn't have wished that feeling on my worst enemy. I was puzzled, trying to figure out how such torment caused by childbirth could possibly be natural.

The midwife finally said to me, "Push. Push and breathe," as if breathing were an option. "Take a deep breath. You're okay. Deeeep breath. Nice and easy," I heard a voice telling me.

My eyes were pinched shut. I hyperventilated right there on the delivery table as I heard, "It's a..." Then, my lids lifted. I wanted to see what was going on.

"Wait!" the midwife prompted.

A doctor then stepped in to take over. "Stop pushing, Tharisse," he said. "Don't push. I need to... Just hold on," was the next command I was given.

I was okay with it for that moment, but then I had to push. I couldn't hold it back. I grunted, "Ughhh!" I pushed one last time, and it was over.

"It's a girl!" was announced aloud in the room by the doctor.

I sighed with relief, and there was the moment I had been eagerly anticipating. However, something was missing. Where was that baby cry I was supposed to hear as they announced the gender? At least, that's what those books I had been reading informed me. I was expecting the glory of holding a slimy little bundle of life against my chest, screaming for breast milk or whatever.

As I laid there catching my breath, I saw a team of white coats come in. Then, my midwife told me, "Just try to relax, so I can stitch your torn vagina."

I wasn't the least bit worried about that. Where was the baby girl they said I had? I asked Jackie, "Where is she? How is she? Why is she not crying?"

Jackie just stood there in the corner of the small and cold delivery room in awe. Then, she came over to me. "She good. They just need to work on her a little bit," she replied.

But what the hell did that mean? I thought. I wanted my baby.

About two endless hours went by, and finally, Jackie came back to me and asked if I was ready.

"Ready for what?" I asked. "Enough of the ready shit, Ma, where is my—"

As I was fixing my lips to completely go off on the nurse that was at my bedside adjusting the IV hookups, I heard a voice say, "Here she is. Here is your little girl."

I tiredly reached my arms out. They placed her little body, tightly wrapped in a white, pink and blue blanket, on my chest. I took my first look at that little, beautiful face poking out from the tiny pink hat sitting snuggly on her head. I couldn't believe, after all the hell we went through, this moment was really happening.

"Hiiiii," I said to my daughter for the first time, and just like I'd seen on TV, I asked her, "So, you're the one who's been kicking me?" I giggled and told her I was a cornball like that. At that moment, she laid there in my arms so peacefully, as if she didn't mind me being corny, at all.

Jackie, who was just as exhausted as I was, said in a frustrated tone, "Okay, I'm leaving now. I will see y'all later."

"Will you call Eugene and let him know the baby is here and that he should get to the hospital ASAP?" I asked Jackie.

Surprisingly, she didn't snap back. She agreed she'd call him.

For the next few minutes, I was a new mother who laid there mesmerized by my little bundle of joy until a nurse came in and took her away again. The midwife came back in to explain to me why they couldn't place my newborn on my chest straight out the womb. It didn't matter to me at that point; I was still flying high off the rush of seeing my newborn daughter for the first time, but apparently, there were some complications.

First, the umbilical cord had wrapped around her little neck. That's why I was told to stop pushing during the delivery; it was so they could unwrap it to prevent strangulation. Secondly, I was so overdue that my little girl began to ingest the fluid as they suspected. The crazy thing was that the baby actually made a bowel movement while still in the womb. Meconium was what she called it.

"We needed to get her lungs drained quickly. You didn't get to see her or hear that little cry you were looking for because the neonatal team of doctors was busy clearing her system to avoid pneumonia." While listening to the midwife, I knew it was evident that my daughter's life was meant to be.

"My daughter fought hard to make it here and messed me up pretty bad in the process, but thank you all for everything," I said.

"I am just happy for you. She is okay; you both are okay," the midwife replied.

Once I was settled in a private room filled with welcoming kits and wash up supplies, I thought I'd get some rest, but a nurse came rolling in with a basket on wheels that contained my little girl, and she was crying. It was music to my ears. The first time I heard my daughter's cry, it was like something triggered in my brain. I felt like her mother.

The nurse asked if I had a name for her yet, and I didn't. I had been pondering a few ideas but hadn't finalized one yet. I told the nurse, "Oh, I am waiting for her father," but that was a lie. The truth was that Eugene didn't have much interest in naming anybody's child. I figured the naming of the baby would happen organically, and it truly did.

As I held my little girl, I steadily looked at her. I began to speak to her as if she could hear and understand what I was saying. I told her that I was so happy to finally meet her.

"Little girl, you have no idea what it took to get you here. I was so sick that I thought I was going to die. I prayed things would be okay, and here you are. I promise you I am going to be the best mother to you. I promise I will always take care of you. Your father is a dumb ass sometimes, but he means well, and you will meet him soon. Just know, it's us against the world. I love you."

Then, her name became obvious. A new life, strong in her spot within my soul. The baby entered a world of the unknown. She was what her mother knew life was going to be about from that moment onward. She was my destiny.

I wasn't the happiest kid in my house for reasons that had yet to be revealed to me, but I was very grateful for the blessing I had just received. I was truly thankful for all my family had done to get her here, but I already knew what my goal was as a mother. I secretly vowed to myself and my newborn daughter not to be anything like the mother I had grown to resent.

On October 8th, 1994, the world welcomed:
Destiny Maliah Washington!

Eugene finally made it to the hospital the next morning and got to see his baby girl for the very first time.

I could tell he was so nervous. He didn't have much to say. I knew him enough to know he was happy and was probably hoping I wouldn't treat him so badly anymore.

Within a couple days, Destiny and I got a clean bill of health, and we were released from the hospital. My aunt came to pick us up, and I was thankful for that as well, seeing as how Eugene couldn't get time off work. Once again, Jackie did an excellent job setting up for us, and she helped me out a lot with Destiny.

I saw a side of my mother that touched me. I informed her I had given her middle name to my daughter as a thank you and appreciation for all she did for us. I guess, in a small way, I hoped Jackie wasn't in as much trouble with Cliff as I grew to suspect. I had reason to believe they had gotten that sniffing of the white substance under control. It may have just been a troubled phase for them. Nevertheless, the dysfunctional family had a new life in the house, and I gained hope that there would possibly be room for some joy.

Time waits for no one, and before I knew it, baby Des was getting older, and life at home continued to change. There were plans to make. I was determined to turn becoming a young mother into the best thing to ever take place in my life. And yes, there was so much for me to learn still, but I saw optimism whenever I looked into my Destiny's eyes.

A future full of possibility awaited us...

CHAPTER THREE
A DEMON HAS INVADED ME

I was nineteen years old on September 5, 1995, a date that always seems like yesterday to me. It was the day I received my death sentence. My induction to death row. I got a letter in the mail stating that I needed to come into the GYN clinic at the local hospital where I had given birth to Destiny just eleven months ago. The letter didn't say why, and I wasn't entirely sure either. I sat there calmly in the crowded waiting area, waiting to be seen.

I was thinking to myself that maybe I had missed a post-baby checkup or something. But, when I got called in by someone who came out of a door that I identified as the "social worker door," I began to worry. I never got called to that door for any of my previous visits. I had been going to that clinic for a while, so it was a bit concerning to me.

I was nervous as hell as I walked toward the lady who called my name. She wore a beautiful Kurti. It was golden-yellow, trimmed in a reddish floral pattern, and hung mid-calf. The red leggings underneath paired well. I don't think I'd ever seen a ponytail as long as hers. I followed her slowly into a small, intimidating room. It had no examination table in it, and clearly, this was a room I did not want to be in. My stomach began to cramp. The room had a no-good-news type of vibe going on. Lots of scattered papers and books and pamphlets. It wasn't bright like an exam room. It was dim, and I could tell it had heard lots of bad news between its walls. She must have noticed the fear written all over my face as my eyes skimmed the room.

"It's going to be okay. Have a seat," she said, as she gently sat down at her unorganized desk. The woman, whose name I had a hard time trying to pronounce, looked down at a blue folder that I'd already noticed lying on top with my name on the tab of it. Just waiting for me. *Go figure!*

She opened the folder. As soon as she parted her lips to speak, my mind suddenly recalled the last conversation I had with Eugene a couple weeks prior.

Without any concern in his tone, he said to me, "Tharisse, I went to a doctor, and he told me I had positive."

"Eugene, what are you talking 'bout?"

His English speaking or comprehension wasn't the best, even after being in the states for a little over ten years.

"Eugene, you told him you had a cold for a few weeks, right?"

He replied, "Yea."

"Okay, so what did he say?"

It didn't seem like Eugene knew for sure what the doctor was telling him. "He told me I had positive and showed me a piece of paper. The doctor said it was a test."

I had no clue what Eugene was trying to say, so I told him to write it for me. "Write down exactly what you saw on the paper, Eugene."

He wrote down +HIV.

I took a deep breath in but forgot to exhale. "Eugene, are you sure he said you had this?"

"Yea, baby, he said I had positive HIV."

I must've asked Eugene about five damn times, "Are you sure that's what he said?"

Eugene acted as if he didn't know what HIV was. I didn't know much other than what I learned from sex education class. During this time, it was still a new illness. I never really thought about it. I definitely didn't know I had to be on the lookout for it.

I told Eugene, if that was what the doctor told him, I wanted to go to that doctor myself and let him tell me directly. "Eugene, it is a disease, and it's a big freakin' deal!"

I needed to know for sure. I wasn't mad at him. I guess I was hoping he was mistaken and that he didn't know what the doctor told him.

Eugene ended up taking me to the doctor he went to, and it turned out to be a clinic at a different hospital than the one I had our daughter. Eugene had to sign papers that gave the doctor permission to talk to me about his care. The staff looked at me funny. Maybe they were wondering why I was there as Eugene's concerned girlfriend. My young appearance, wearing a t-shirt and jeans and standing with a man who was considerably older than me, should have raised a red flag.

After talking with the doctor, it turned out Eugene was right; he had tested HIV positive. The mature Tharisse stepped up. Rather than walking the hell up out of there, I took a deep breath and stayed to discuss the next steps for Eugene with the doctors.

I left the doctor's office with Eugene feeling horrified, my stomach in knots, bile rising in my throat over what I had just heard. Eugene and I didn't speak to each other at all during the drive home. I'm not sure how he felt, but I was scared. I sat rigidly in the car as I went over the next steps and all my options. The first thing that needed to be done, of course, was exactly what the doctor had recommended. I had to get myself and Destiny tested.

I realized then, as I sat in front of this well-attired woman who was giving me a look of sympathy and pity, the letter I received in the mail telling me to come into my clinic must've had something to do with the test I requested as a result of what Eugene's doctor told me.

I had no idea I'd actually be sitting in an office with a social worker being told, "Ms. Washington, we have the results from the HIV antibody testing you requested. You have tested HIV positive." Every word made the lump in my throat grow bigger and bigger.

My first response was, "But, I just had a baby. What about her?"

"She'll need to be tested too."

My tears were stuck. They were in shock.

Sitting there trying to swallow, my mouth having suddenly gone dry, I asked, "How am I supposed to tell my mother some shit like this?"

Warm tears trickled down my face. I wasn't sure why they were falling though, because as I sat there, I felt my mind go blank. My body went completely numb. I really didn't know what to feel. I didn't know how to feel.

"Is there someone I can call for you, dear?" the elegantly dressed social worker asked me.

I replied, "No, I'm okay." I was in shock just like my tears. I wasn't fine. I was scared.

That woman who had just changed my life continued with her explanation. "There are medications available that would allow you to live a full, productive life. Although there isn't currently a cure for the virus, with a strong treatment plan, healthy diet, and emotional support, testing positive for HIV doesn't necessarily mean you are being given a death sentence."

All I heard was *blah blah blah.* The room I saw so vividly upon entering suddenly disappeared. I felt like I was sitting on the edge of a tall cliff. It felt cold like the delivery room where I gave birth to Destiny. I could smell the scent of the first day of school—autumn air. My body was tight. All I could think to do was hold still. I was afraid to make any moves because it felt like some force was trying to push me over the edge. I just sat in disbelief. How could she have said all those things when the image of this sickness was of those who were dying off fast and suffering?

As encouraging as it was meant to come off, that was exactly what I had interpreted her words to be that day. A death sentence. I felt a fear so deep placed within me. Who would have thought on that dreary, gray day, with the rain pouring down, my very first encounter with Eugene, one of those clustered dark clouds would follow me for the rest of my life?

The days following that unimaginable diagnosis felt like an ache in my heart that was bound to become an unbearable pain. It was a recurring thought, unexpected like an uninvited guest. A demon had invaded me. I couldn't process anything anyone said to me. I isolated myself in my room for a good two weeks or so. My thoughts of not wanting to face the future weeks ahead became constant, and it was those very thoughts that led me to believe I had lost any will of having a life to look forward to. I lost all hope.

Destiny was the nucleus of my soul. The beat of my heart. It made things that much more difficult to face. How would I raise this daughter with all the love and nourishment of my existence? Everything I had ever believed could be was ripped right out of me. On that dreadful day that I received the diagnosis, I became this fearful little girl. I was placed in unfamiliar territory. Every step I took had to be taken carefully. I didn't know where I was headed or where I would end up.

It was almost a month later when it all began to really sink in. As much as I tried to go about life as if nothing was wrong, my mom was taking notice of my mood. It was time to conquer the first battle. I told Jackie the news I received.

"Ma, I don't know how to say this. Please, don't go off on me."

"Girl, what the hell you talking 'bout now?"

"Eugene told me he tested HIV positive." Speaking those words felt like spitting fire. It hurt.

"What you mean?"

The dusty rainbow throw rug on my bedroom floor became my focal point. Each color seemed to represent a life I thought I would have had at some point. *We all dream, right? Well, my dreams were destroyed by a diagnosis.*

"He's sick. I spoke to his doctor already. I went and got tested too, Ma."

She interrupted, "And?"

My mouth was so dry, but the words found their way through. "And, I am sick too."

I couldn't even look up at my mother. I continued to look down at my colors of life. I was afraid to see what her face showed.

To my surprise, Jackie's response was not as intense as expected. In fact, Jackie reacted totally opposite, as if she didn't believe what I had just told her. Almost like there was no such thing as her daughter being HIV positive.

I needed to hear her say something. She could have said, "Oh my goodness" or "What the hell?" or "Give me a hug!" or even "Imma kill that muthafucka!" Something... Anything... But there was nothing. No tears shed between us, no hugs of endearment, no reassurance that everything would be okay. My mother must have been in shock too.

At the time I figured, if my mom could actually form the words, she would have said all those things. She would have said more. My mother was definitely capable of cursing up a storm to get her point across.

That night, I took the baby, and we went and stayed the night at Eugene's place. I still had to have the same damn talk with him. I needed a good meal that night to pretend that this shit was not happening. I acquired that skill without being aware of it; I pretended everything was alright when, in fact, it wasn't.

There was this little Spanish joint on Park Avenue in Newark that Eugene introduced me to. It had the best yellow rice with red beans and fried pork. It always made me happy when I ate it so that's what we got to eat. After my dinner, I hardly had much to say; I just wanted to go to sleep and savor that one happy moment. Des slept through the night in between us. It was a good evening.

The next morning, we all woke up, and I knew speaking with the man, who at that time I believed had stolen my life, was something that needed to be done. I asked Eugene to go to work late so that we could talk.

Before I lost my nerve, I said, "I went to have my test done." When the words managed to depart my quivering lips, something ignited in me.

The moment I saw the clueless look on his face, I didn't give him a chance to respond to my statement. I lashed out at him. I tried to knock his ass clear across that studio apartment as if I could really beat on him, or anyone for that matter. I was not an intentionally violent person, but given the circumstances, I couldn't control myself. Another force had taken over.

Exposing my daughter to any type of domestic violence was something I promised to never do. I didn't want her to grow up having nightmares similar to those of my own. It was the first promise I broke as a parent. I punched and slapped with all my might.

"You son of a bitch!" I threw anything within my reach. "What the hell are we supposed to do now, Eugene?"

Dishes flew, the TV remote flew, and his clothes went flying every which way in that little apartment. I struggled to catch my breath, shouting and choking on my spit. My face smeared with tears and snot.

"I can't believe you did this to meeee!" I shrieked. I was crying so hard everything became a blur.

I grabbed Des, threw on her jacket, and stormed out the door and down the stairs. She began to cry. The people in the apartment underneath were peeking out their door as I passed by. The woman asked me, "Is everything alright, honey?"

I rudely ignored her. I went outside and rested on the porch and couldn't stop my mind from wandering. I started to think about Eugene and what went wrong and when. *How did this shit happen?*

All I could hear was him saying, "I never get sick. I never get a cold. I'm strong."

"Bullshit!" I muttered to myself.

Eugene was this soft guy, with a big heart and meek voice. Frankly, I didn't give a fuck about any of that at that moment. I was young and thought I'd found my one. He was my first official boyfriend. Eugene was fortunate to have me as his girl. I was intelligent and mature beyond my years and had a big heart just like him; although, at times I struggled to believe that. So, despite my anger about having contracted this illness from the father of my only child, I continued to love him. Our relationship continued. It was something inside my heart that felt like I shouldn't turn my back on him. He needed me to support him.

Honestly, I don't know what in the world I was thinking, or it could be I wasn't thinking at all. Who was gonna support me? Who was gonna look out for our daughter?

What bothered me the most was that Jackie told me more than once, "Tharisse, there is something that just rubs me the wrong way about him." Those were here exact words. My mom was right the whole time. If I would have just listened to her back then, maybe I could have avoided being robbed of my self-worth.

The next few months consisted of doctor visits for both me and Eugene. We tried to get educated on what was to come. I decided against further medical treatment after they gave me AZT. It was the go-to viral therapy at the time, but it made me sick as hell. I was not about to have HIV meds making me feel worse than I initially did without them. I definitely didn't want those pills lying around, reminding me of my condition. Physically, I felt fine. The bigger issue I faced was baby Des still hadn't been tested. It was like the sickness was growing in existence, despite my efforts to hide from it. I fought against those thoughts of being futureless. I had to fight to move on. Live life with the virus.

Destiny received all HIV negative results from her testing at the ages of one-year-old and every three months until she was two years old. Waiting for those results to come in, I swear it gave me gray hair. Her pediatrician determined she was in the clear at that point, and I needed not to worry myself any more about having her tested again, except in the event Destiny was exposed to it by not taking all necessary precautionary measures. After all, she was being raised by infected parents.

Knowing my daughter was HIV negative was like a warm blanket during a winter night and a refreshing drink in the desert. And I cherished it. I appreciated God looking out for Destiny as he had always done since the beginning of her conception. I made sure I was extra cautious while caring for her. That's probably when I first started showing signs of OCD. I would always make sure everything she touched was wiped down with bleach first. I would especially pay attention to my hands when preparing food, making sure not to cut myself. I would constantly wash Destiny's face and hands. Spraying Lysol on anything I touched.

This behavior was often mistaken as typical new mother behavior to the outside world. In my head, I knew the personal reasons surrounding my actions. So, those practices became habitual in my world. Even though Des was growing older, it was completely unknown that there was a problem developing.

After her birth, I realized how much of a blessing she was. I had actually been given a destiny I unconsciously yearned for. It was something precious; I knew my gift of motherhood had to be carefully handled, too.

As someone who loved her child beyond what words could ever describe, I was terribly angry inside. I thought I had to protect Des from me, her own mother. There were times I wanted to kiss my baby and wouldn't because I thought I would be endangering her. I gave her little kisses on her cheek, but when Des would try and kiss her mommy on the lips, I turned away from her. She always looked at me disappointedly, as if I rejected her. My heart broke into smaller pieces every single time. It made me cry sometimes just thinking about the last time I kissed my little girl on her little lips. It was before I knew my diagnosis, but how was I to know it would be the last time?

It seemed like the pages of the calendar turned progressively quick. Days became weeks and weeks turned into months, and I was still amongst the living.

I had just about all I could take living at home with parents who were so into their own thing they wouldn't have noticed us gone anyhow. It was like they wanted us there but didn't. Good days at home became nothing more than occasionally. I went back to school and got my high school diploma and found a part-time job. I was finally providing for my daughter financially, along with the help of her father, of course. So, Eugene and I decided it was time to move me out of my parents' house.

I was saddened to leave my younger siblings, but I had to make moves. At the end of the day, I was their big sister and felt like I had to look out for them as if they were my own kids. I knew in my heart that I would go and get myself set up nicely and have them come over on the weekends or whenever they wanted to. I had hoped they'd be alright. I mean, they did have their mother and father looking after them, so they stood a better chance than I ever did. At least, that's how I always felt. I had my Destiny to think about, and she was my priority at the time. I needed to make sure she was surrounded by as much positive energy and love one could ever have.

So, I did it. I moved in with Eugene in his small bachelor pad apartment, which I'd always have to tidy up. Somehow, the dirty work uniforms and smelly socks managed to scatter themselves all over the place despite my housekeeping efforts. The microwave and toaster oven he used more than the actual stovetop needed to be trashed. The bathroom had no tub; it was just a shower. I explained to Eugene that his apartment wasn't the ideal place to raise our daughter.

He was unsure at first, but that following month, Eugene came to me. "Honey, I got a better place for you."

"Uh, that was kind of fast. Why didn't you let me see it first?" I asked him, but rather than waste *more* time trying to figure out why, I just went along with Eugene's plans.

We moved into a bigger apartment, and I was able to furnish it and set things up the way I wanted to. We had a dark-green pleather sofa that was comfy and cozy. The tall corner faux plant fitted nicely with the rest of the traditional home décor palette I had created. I kept the hardwood floors waxed, just as I learned from my mom. Our kitchen was small, yet efficient with basic white appliances. There was some apple patterned, stale wallpaper in there. Our bedroom had a full-sized mattress set that had no frame or headboard. It sat flat to the floor. Destiny had her very own Little Tykes™ bed and a toy chest to match. It was so cute and pink, perfect for our princess. I filled the rooms with knick-knacks from a local thrift store. I was excited to be starting this new life with this man, the father of my child. I buried the diagnosis. I focused on the moment.

I knew Eugene would still be looking for sex. I would put two condoms on him whenever I chose to be bothered with him intimately. Strangely, I felt the need to protect myself from him, even though the damage had already been done. I remembered thinking that maybe the lab made a mistake, and if I showed God I had learned my lesson, it would somehow change the results.

Nonetheless, Destiny was going to be raised by two parents that were willing to do whatever it took to see to it that their daughter was the main factor in the equation that equaled a family. She would be raised with principles and morals and not by circumstance. At least, that's what I set my mind to think. Love and attention wouldn't be something that Destiny would ever have to question or seek out from us. I had my own little family that was on its way to being everything I had always dreamed of from such a young age.

I had always seen myself with lots of children and a healthy marriage with a big home that would get filled with so much love. My maternal grandma's traditions would've carried on in that home I'd create myself, and some would have hopefully carried on into Destiny's family. I would have a career, and my husband would have his own business, which Eugene was working towards. So yes, we were definitely on our way. I created this fantasy and, no matter what, I was going to see it through.

My mom, Jackie, was so opinionated to the point that when she and my stepfather, who was one that didn't think before he spoke, came to check out our first apartment, they basically made me feel like I hadn't accomplished shit and that the place Eugene had chosen was not good enough to raise a kid. I was already expecting to hear the worse from them, but sometimes you can't help but hope for something different. Even though my apartment with Eugene and Destiny wasn't exactly luxurious in style, it didn't matter much. I couldn't remember ever living in any apartments that were much different growing up, regardless of how Jackie and Cliff reacted.

But, these were the parents that I had, and they were entitled to voice their thoughts and opinions. If I was gonna bury the realization of the illness that plagued my life, then I might as well put my negative feelings toward my parents in that same dark place. It was the only way to tolerate it all.

My life was moving in a direction that I considered better than no direction at all, and for that, I was grateful. I even met a wonderful woman at my office job I had gotten while finishing up my senior year in high school.

Cora was this sweet, older lady, very religious, and spiritually mature. She befriended me and was impressed with how eager I was to learn all there was to learn about the business we were working for. Cora even taught me some bookkeeping skills and allowed me to assist her with those duties.

I never understood how I was able to capture this woman's heart, but needless to say, Cora grew to love me. She guided me back into the church life and even encouraged my baptism. We were spiritually connected. Cora became my mother through Christ, my godmother. I felt this lady was special because she actually took an interest in me and enjoyed spending time with me and teaching me.

Over time, she let me drive her car and welcomed me into her home. Cora had no children of her own. She was proud to call me her daughter and was tickled pink by the personality Destiny had developed. Even though Jackie was my biological mother, and I loved her, Cora played the part very well, and I loved her for that.

I eventually confided in Cora and told her about my illness. She was caught off guard but assured me that because I chose to put Christ as the leader in my life, I would be fine.

Her love for me didn't change one bit. After getting over her shock, she said, "Tharisse, I don't know why you came into my life, but I am a believer in God's work. I knew from the day I met you, there was something special inside of you. God aligned us, and I know you're a good girl."

"Thank you, Cora, for being who you are," I said.

She replied, "Tharisse, promise me you will never give up."

I then assured her by saying, "I promise, god-momma, I promise."

That day, after I promised her, we cried and prayed some more.

If it weren't for being saved, I might not have seen the days ahead. I had decided to put God first in everything I did. Reinforced by my faith, I chose to keep that demon hibernated. I continued to focus on my daughter and making each and every day count for anything worth living for; anything normal is what I began to strive for. If I was blessed with an opportunity to teach Destiny something, then I wanted to do just that.

My mindset shifted. I began my mission to steer my Destiny in the direction I felt would mold her into the perfect woman. I knew realistically there was no such thing as a "perfect" person, other than Jesus, but in my mind, a timeline had begun, and our life was under construction. So, I knew there was no time to waste. My daughter had to have a blueprint to follow to guide her in building this "not-quite-perfect" perfect life.

CHAPTER FOUR
EUGENE

The music of Mary J. Blige's *What's the 411©* CD played while riding around the streets of Newark. Cruising through Weequahic Park eating White Castle became nothing more than memories after Destiny was born, and even more distant after finding out we both were sick.

My suppressed reality made its way back to the surface when Eugene's health declined very quickly. He decided to go through it without me. He felt like I had my hands full with our daughter. He wanted me to center my energy on Des. Eugene told me out of his own mouth that he wanted me to take care of his baby *for* him. It was unclear to me how he could make such a request as the father, but I later came to understand the actual meaning behind those words.

It was a typical day. I was at home with Des, waiting for Eugene to come in from work. I had cooked dinner: beef steak with white potatoes and carrots. I waited, and the night became morning. Eugene never showed. I immediately went into panic mode and called the auto shop where he worked.

Ron, the owner, said, "He didn't come in today, darling."

"Okay, thanks. If he shows up, have him call me, please."

Full of worry, I began calling the hospitals. Lastly, I called his only sister, Lisa. She said she hadn't seen or heard from him either. At that point, I didn't know what to think. I tried my best to remain calm, wishing he would come through the door at any moment. He never did. Days went by and still no sign of Eugene. His sister showed up early one morning, unannounced, and asked me if he'd called yet. I felt she was withholding something.

"Lisa, if you know something, just spill it. I'm in no mood to play games. I'm here in this apartment, and I got my baby to think about. Don't do this, please."

Lisa said, "You know Eugene is sick. You know he loves you."

I said, "Of course, I know he is sick. Did he tell you I'm sick, too? Did ya' brotha tell you that? Whatever!"

Hearing her words bore an effect on me, but what I saw when I looked at her was him, just a lighter version. Eugene was of a darker complexion, and she was lighter. They both had larger lips and full noses. They had dark eyes. Bright, aligned teeth that resembled those you would see in toothpaste commercials. I was frazzled. She wasn't.

She went on to say, "He left. He left 'cause he was sick."

"Are you kidding me?" My insides were hot, but my lips were quivering. "What the hell you talking 'bout he left?"

I began getting Destiny dressed as I looked at this lady like 'you betta get outta here with that bullshit.' My daughter, without a clue as to what we were saying, seemed just as shook. Maybe something within her own young spirit felt a shift in what was becoming a life without her dad.

Without entertaining that nonsense any further, I told her, "Listen here, I'm about to leave and go to my mom's house, so if you hear from ya' brotha again, tell him to burn in hell!" I tried holding back my tears. "Let him know I'm leaving this apartment."

I was probably disrespectful toward her, but I didn't care. I called a cab. Then, I heard the door open and close. I rushed out of the bedroom.

"Is that... Oh."

She had left. What was I gonna do now?

I said to myself, "Okay, Tharisse, keep it together. You got this." But, I didn't think I actually had anything but another fucked up situation to get through. Just thinking about it gave me a massive headache.

My cab came, and I headed to my parents' house. It was mid-morning, so I rang the doorbell. Cliff answered the door and immediately swooped Destiny from my arms.

"What you doing here, girl?" he asked me as if I needed a particular reason to come there.

"I need my mother, Cliff. Hey, Ma, I think Eugene left and went back to his country."

My mother stood at the kitchen sink washing dishes. "Tharisse, what the hell? What you mean *left?*"

I told her he hadn't been home for a few days, and Lisa had dropped by the house earlier that day to tell me he chose to leave.

"'Cause he was sick. Like okay, I'm sick too, so what do he think this is?" I was heated.

My mother looked at me as if I were speaking another language besides clear English. She wiped her forehead with the back of her hand like she was fed up. "Tharisse, enough of this sick shit already. What are you going to do?" I sensed the mom in her was coming to my rescue. She continued to say, "You know you got that baby now, and nobody got time for the dumb shit, okay? You gotta get your shit together 'cause you need to take care of yourself so you can take care of your daughter."

I fought my tears from building up in my eyes. My mother showed up. She must've known I needed to hear from her. I couldn't remember what it was like to be loved by my mother. I liked the fuzzy feeling her words gave me. If my mom could bear to actually speak those words to me, then I needed to do just as she said.

Damn it! She was right about Eugene. Unbelievable. I was an adult and was finally ready to listen to my mother. I was in a tough spot, and the more I thought about it, the more pissed off I got all over again.

After talking with my mother, she convinced me to stay the night. She said she would go with me the next day and help me start packing up the apartment. I wasn't gonna try to keep it without Eugene. If I had to move on without him, then I needed a fresh slate. I didn't want to move back home with my family. I had my own family, even though Eugene broke it. Even though he broke us. Even though he shattered me.

That next day, while at the apartment organizing some stuff, I called my godmother, Cora, to fill her in on what was going on.

She said, "Oh, my Lord, I am so sorry."

That just made me feel worse. Cora and I didn't necessarily speak every day, but I always knew she was there for me when I needed her.

I didn't want her to worry about me, so I put on my best voice filled with false bravado and told her, "It's crazy, right? But, at least I didn't run. I stuck around for him. Maybe he wasn't strong enough, and thought he was doing me a favor, right?"

Who was I kidding? I was human, and I was mad as hell.

"So, yea, don't worry about me. My mother is with me now, helping me figure this all out. Just pray for me. Ya' kno'? It will all work out, right? I love you, God-momma."

"I love you too, Tharisse."

Mixed with emotions, I was glad to have Jackie help me through this. Sometimes, I looked at her like an evil witch, but that was still my mom, and sometimes, in her small little way, she let me know she really did love me. I decided to take a Christ-like approach to life and all it had to offer. Appreciating the good, learning from the bad, and realizing that people aren't perfect, not even my parents.

While life was beginning to show me just how beautiful it could be by blessing me with my daughter, it was also revealing the not so pretty things. Already, I had to grow up fast when I became a young mom, but with everything else that had transpired: being diagnosed with HIV and Eugene leaving, I needed to grow up a little more. And do it even faster than before.

In the midst of everything, I opted to start a diary. It was always cool when I watched the after-school specials, and the teen girls would have their diaries under their mattress or wherever. They would have a place to keep their deepest feelings. I figured why not create my own secret place, too. Lord knows, I had some harsh shit in my head that needed to be sorted out. At least, I didn't have to worry about my little brother finding it and exposing me to my friends for blackmail because we didn't live together.

That day, as I sat in my new apartment with my brand-new journal, I laughed to myself softly, even as I wrote my first entry. I just went for it. I dove right in.

Dear Diary,

Being so angry that it takes over who I truly aspired to be isn't supposed to be in my cards. A mother with an exciting future ahead positively impacting the world in some way would be nice. Maybe, a world traveler. My outlook on everything in life has become negative. Endless possibilities stored away, absent of their meanings. I feel incapable of seeing the good—the beauties of the universe—and the light at the end of my tunnel appears so dim that I question whether it is there at all. The distance of that tunnel has no ending, yet, some days I feel hopeful that the light will eventually expose itself. But mostly, I am convinced that there is no truth to a light waiting at all.

I am enraged that my life has turned into a damn mockery. I am still so young. Aren't I supposed to be happy and living life to the fullest? How did I get hit with all of this so soon? I am often told through the Word that I have to be satisfied with what God has given me and how he has created me just as I should be. But I am confused. I am so lost. Please, I am begging you, Lord, help me understand.

As a result of Eugene's abandonment, I fell into a slight depression. A healing heart broken again. I quit my part-time job and was left homeless for several months. There was never an invite from my parents to come back home. A small part of me was okay with that. My mom still did what she could to help Des and me. She'd give us a few dollars here and there; sometimes, I didn't have to ask. She would also babysit Destiny while I worked.

We ended up on welfare, and they helped us get our own place. After spending about ten long weeks in the Newark YMCA during the dead of winter weather, I was so ready to be out of there. I could remember the sidewalks of downtown Newark being so icy and slippery. I bust my ass a few times. Luckily, I was never injured, or I might have sued somebody's ass as desperate for money as I was.

What I learned most by that experience of homelessness was that, when you have to depend on assistance from the state, try your damnedest to keep it to a minimum. Those in charge of those places didn't seem to care much about the conditions of them. Cracked, leaky ceilings, bedbugs and worn cots disguised as beds were a few conditions I prayed could be better. It was a horrific experience, but I managed to keep going. I wasn't sure how, but I did.

To that end, we looked forward to our very own place. I found a one-bedroom apartment in a roach infested, rodent-filled building. It was far from fancy, but it was a huge deal to me, my first accomplishment without the help of Eugene.

It wasn't long after moving into that apartment that I began to wonder about him. After all this time, he randomly popped into my mind. I was still angry, but I also still loved him. I worried about him.

When Des was about three-years-old, it was a Sunday, and we were just laying around in our partially furnished living room. We had a small couch where we chilled often.

The multicolored, coarse fabric wasn't comfortable, but I'd put a blanket in between us and it. The dingy, pale, yellow walls were bare only wearing their aged, crackled paint. The wind was blowing really hard outside. I couldn't resist when a strange feeling came over me.

"Destiny, get your boots on, baby."

"Okay, mommy, where we goin'?"

I didn't answer her; I simply ordered her to get her jacket.

"Mommy, where we goin'?" She asked a lot of questions at the tender age of three.

I took Des to the payphone across the street from our building to call Eugene's sister. I wanted to reach out to her since I hadn't spoken to her since our last encounter.

Why would I open up an old wound such as this? I asked myself. I guessed maybe missing Eugene was normal, even though in my imaginary mind, he was this big bad wolf that had basically blown our house down.

I stood at the payphone, and the wind damn near blew me over. Des was chasing the leaves around. She loved stomping them to hear the crunching sound.

I swallowed deeply when Lisa answered the phone. "Uh, hello, it's Tharisse."

"Hi, how you doing?" She seemed unbothered by my call.

"Have you heard from Eugene lately?" I asked.

She spoke to me as if the past couple of years hadn't happened. She began telling me about her recent trip to Haiti. I unexpectedly felt another life-changing shift happening. The earth seemed to have moved around me.

I yelled out to Des, "Get ya' ass ova here, girl!"

Lisa asked, "How is your daughter?"

"She is good." I grabbed my baby girl close. I needed her for comfort. I heard the hesitation and distress in Lisa's voice. It was the same unease that had crawled its way up my spine and compelled me to call her.

On that windy autumn afternoon in October of 1997, Lisa told me that the love of my life, the father of my only child, was dead.

"Ummmm," was all I kept repeatedly saying as the tears slowly ran down my chilled face. Each tear seemed to bring a memory of the times he and I spent together. My tongue was heavy. The sadness blocked all communication signals. I couldn't form any other words at the time.

Lisa could tell I was obviously heartbroken by the news. The next thing she said was, "Take care, Tharisse, and take care of that little girl," as if I needed to hear that shit one more time.

And, so there we were, Destiny and I, standing by a public payphone, stuck in an awful moment of time. Little

Destiny's hand in mine, I felt like everybody and everything that existed in the world had suddenly disappeared. We just stood there looking lost like we were left alone in the world all over again. Me and my Destiny.

I took Des back in the house and sat on the couch. A twilight zone experience had abducted me. The next thing I knew, it was several days later, and my mom was banging on the door. As one can imagine, after spending days on the couch with a toddler running around, the cleanliness of the place was unacceptable, but I didn't care. I had experienced an aftershock of the earthquake that occurred the day I received my "death sentence." Finding out Eugene was dead gave me confirmation of what I was to expect at any given time.

My mother barged in. She asked me what my problem was. "Why haven't you called me to let me know you guys were okay, Tharisse? You know you don't have a damn phone for me to call you. And, why does it look as if you and Des have been sleeping in the living room?"

"Maaaaa! Okay, okay!" I tried to find the words to explain. Barely able to speak, I gazed at my daughter, who was eating cereal straight out the box, and softly mumbled, "Her father died."

Jackie looked at me with that same face. It harbored confusion, anger, and fear. Each time I had more news to report, my mom got worse at hiding how she truly felt. She was in just as much pain as I was.

The demon had resurfaced. I knew I had to say it. I had to speak the words aloud, not just so Jackie could understand me, but also for my own understanding. Loudly, angrily, certainly with a convincing attitude, I repeated the scary truth. "HER FATHER DIED! I CALLED LISA A FEW DAYS AGO, JUST TO CHECK IN. MA, SHE TOLD ME HE DIED. THE BASTARD INFECTED ME WITH HIS HIV, AND THEN HE GOES AND DIES. HE LEFT US. HE LEFT MY DAUGHTER, OUR DAUGHTER."

My mother slowly made her way to the door. I noticed her lips were parted, but I heard nothing. Her red tinted eyes deepened with moisture. She walked out of the apartment without even saying goodbye.

I had no choice but to bury that demon, yet again. It would have been detrimental if I hadn't. Keeping the demon locked away and pretending it didn't exist was my only way to function. My daughter didn't even know what was going on. She lost a father she would never know, just as she was losing a mother, all she'd ever known.

After Jackie left, I gave Destiny a nice, warm bubble bath in my lavender scented body wash, which was considered to be calming, but I was the one who really needed to be soothed.

After her bath, I made us cheeseburgers and tater tots to eat. Des liked those. We laid on the couch together and watched *Barney* ™ on TV. I was internally contemplating my next move. My mom and I hardly ever spoke of that forbidden topic again.

The years I raised Destiny seemed to have flown by. I kept the thought of it all buried deep inside, careful not to allow it to seep out through the crevices of my broken soul. I wanted to focus on day-to-day life, and it wasn't much to it. I got a job at a fast food restaurant and became a shift manager rather quickly. I worked tirelessly. I prayed on the regular. I educated Destiny about life on a daily basis, so worried that my time with her would run out on us. Destiny needed me. There was a damned if you do, damned if you don't world that was waiting for her.

Life had to go on. I spent the next few years working really hard. I lasted about three years at that job. During my employment there, I formed an intimate relationship with a coworker; it didn't end well. He was an easy distraction. After suffering through the loss of Eugene, I needed to try to feel again. But, this guy had commitment issues, so I went full speed ahead into a rude awakening.

When I realized this guy wasn't the "it" I wanted, things spiraled out of control.

He rejected my unpredictable actions. The not knowing who I had become began. I guess I wasn't sure about how to love again. I learned the harsh lessons of infidelity and the impact it has on self-image. Both of us had become guilty of creeping. I grew more depressed, and my behavior reflected my mood. The beginning of falling in love all over again concluded in being forced out of love.

Furthermore, jumping in and out of relationships became routine. I was in search of the next 'love thang,' a potential happily ever after, even though I knew I was damaged goods. I had a secret I didn't share with anyone, and I thought I was okay with that.

My diary became overloaded with words of sadness.

Dear Diary,

I know negativity. I know feelings of despair, frustration, anger and just an overall feeling of less than. I know these oh so well. Some may call it depression, and that may have been so, but to the contrary. I also know love, joy, hope, and faith; those positive feelings we all yearn for. So, what would you define that as?

When you are blessed with having more than one perception of life, the ability to relate to others on a multitude of levels, having those experiences that totally justify the see-saw of emotions, you often wonder where exactly you fit in. And then, one day you find yourself with nothing else, just those thoughts of what, why, and how. Something deep gives comfort knowing that maybe, just maybe, all of it is for the good of another. Are there others out there trapped in their own darkness? I ask you Lord, please help me push through. Please, help me do right by others as I would have them do unto me.

Faking the funk became my way of life. I had no choice but to pretend all was well. It wasn't. There was too much at stake; so much that had already ruined me. Through those moments, I scarcely held on.

I was always on the lookout for the next step that could gain Destiny and I a better life. I somehow began to dream again. Having that big house, nicely decorated, and having family gatherings for the holidays. I even had thoughts of becoming a foster parent one day. There was something about motherhood that was exciting to me. When I was younger, I used to babysit little cousins on the weekends. I loved the idea of playing mommy. Reminiscing on those dreams usually put a smile on my face. I was determined to contain my pain.

Destiny was growing into this very special little girl. It was apparent that one day she would make a big mark in the world, and I began to notice it.

I saw the small things that every mother should but sometimes doesn't. Destiny was very talkative; she described things in so much detail. Her thoughts were forming into stories, and she didn't mind sharing them. She enjoyed watching TV and even memorized the dialogue from her favorite shows and movies. Destiny took a particular liking to horror movies, and she reenacted scenes. It was the funniest thing to see this little girl acting and pretending to be afraid and imitating the actors in those movies. Destiny seemed to have a gift when it came to acting, and she was naturally dramatic.

"Mommy, lemme show you! Lemme show you!"

"Show me what, girl?"

She demanded my attention. "Look!"

"Okay, I see you, Des." I watched her closely, and the child would be crying all of a sudden, for no reason.

"Baby, what's wrong? What happened?" As her mother, I was genuinely concerned.

She'd laugh at me. "Mommy, see, I told you I could cry."

I called her my little drama queen and left it at that.

I took note; it was going to be an interesting ride watching my Destiny grow up. I almost feared what her adolescent stage would be like. I hoped she wasn't out of control like me. I had to work especially hard to see to it that Destiny was molded and trained to be respectful to herself. I had to make sure she learned early there were serious consequences for certain decisions and choices made in life.

Time moved forward for the two us, the pressures of managing all the responsibilities overwhelming at times. Although I was in no way intimidated by life's obstacles, I continued learning that things weren't as easy as I previously assumed. Life lessons hit me left and right.

Dear Diary,

Ever wonder how your upbringing will play a significant part in the adult you become?

Regardless of how, just know that it will. Maybe I shouldn't have been so hard on my parents. I mean, my mother did her best, I suppose. She and my stepfather never intentionally hurt us. They made sure we ate and had a roof over our heads and clean clothes on our backs. The basic responsibilities of a parent. My perception of them is changing slightly. I am convinced that being a parent has its tough moments. I am still a work in progress.

Lord, please help me see what you want me to see.

Unbreak My Heart by Kashinda T. Marche

CHAPTER FIVE
AM I CRAZY?

I was a bonafide go-getter. I worked hard and was able to move Destiny and me into a decent suburban neighborhood. She was six years old. It had a great school system. I hoped Destiny would thrive. The years sped by. There were periods when I worked around the clock—times when I felt the world was this place that had no rules. Money meant nothing to me anymore. I was making plenty of it until that other side of me showed up, and my energy levels would plummet.

As a result, there were times when I didn't work at all. I couldn't even get out of bed. I suffered from major mood swings. Periodic depressive behavior resurfaced again and again. I became a person I no longer recognized. Two people were living inside of me, and I had a hard time figuring out who the real me was.

As far as I knew, my daughter was okay. She was intelligent with exceptional grades in school. She was a social butterfly. As a parent, I was as proud as I could possibly be. People always praised the wonderful job I was doing raising her. They didn't know the struggle it took to present such a nice image. I'd often think to myself, *am I really doing that great of a job?*

It seemed Destiny and I were going through normal stuff, and everything was as it should be. She would have her moments of defiance, and I would have to discipline her. I never came down too hard on my daughter; at least, I didn't think I did. I would bounce in and out of the highs and lows. And, Destiny was bounced right along, too. I became more unpredictable.

My mother would often say, "Girl, you must be losing your mind. You need to get ya' shit together and stop acting like a damn fool."

She was right; I felt like I was losing it.

The older Destiny got, the more I started to notice how much my daughter was absorbing from me. It frightened me. I didn't know what to do or if there was anything to do. She began showing signs of anxiety: biting her nails and procrastinating on her house chores. She became argumentative with me. I took it as that normal stuff we went through, only later to find out things weren't what they seemed to be. The life of Destiny and I together was one thing, unaware of the individuals we also were.

One day, I walked into the house from a doctor's appointment. I called out to her, "Des, you home yet?" I got no response. I opened her bedroom door and almost fell to the floor because of what I saw. Confused, I asked, "What the hell? Little girl, what is going on? Who the hell?"

My eleven-year-old daughter was laid across her bed with a boy, apparently from her school. They were watching a movie, fully clothed, thank the Lord; however, I couldn't get past the fact that there was an unknown friend, more importantly, a boy, in my daughter's bed.

Nonchalantly, he said to me, "Hi, Ms. Washington."

I was stuck. I had to find the appropriate words for this boy.

"Little boy, if you don't get your ass out that bed! As a matter of fact, if you don't get your ass out my house!"

Destiny had the nerve to say, "Maaaaa, stop being rude to my friend. We just watching TV. You got friends you lay with."

She'd struck a nerve with me. I was lost for words again.

That boy learned with the quickness that my tight-lipped expression meant serious business. He put his sneakers on and went to scurry out. He quickly said goodbye to Destiny before leaving, "See you in school, Destiny." Then, he muttered to me, "Sorry, Ms. Washington."

"How could you possibly think this was okay?" I asked her.

Without waiting for an answer, I went into my room and slammed my door. I had to walk away because I was two seconds from whooping that ass. A part of me felt I had no right given my own behavior. It became clear parenting had no script. We must learn as we grow, with the hopes of growing at all.

I rarely had to put my hands on Destiny as a form of chastisement. We usually talked things through when issues came about, but I kind of felt that I was to blame. My recent conduct hadn't exactly been a good example.

My behavior was affecting my child, and I mistakenly ignored it as normal child behavior. Destiny and I had an extremely close relationship; we were strongly bonded. I figured as long as we remained openly communicative, she would verbally express to me if I were doing something wrong or if she was being hurt in any way. But, how could I expect my child to know the difference if I didn't?

My choices, decisions, and behavior were indeed setting a negative example in Destiny's life. My judgment was altered by my emotional/mental disorder, and it was consequently hurting us. I was clueless about it all. I'd sometimes ask her questions like, "Des, is everything alright with you? Is everything okay with us? How are things in school?"

She would always respond, "Yup, everything is okay, mommy. Are you okay?"

I'd reply, "Yup, I'm fine, and all is good, baby." I was obviously lying to her and to myself.

At different points in my life, I gave therapy a shot and had even been on various medications to treat depression and anxiety. I never committed to it long term, which left my mental illness untreated. I experienced the ride of an emotional rollercoaster for most of my life. I often wondered if my siblings ever noticed changes in me. If so, they never spoke about it.

Some of the issues I attempted to work out were the losses I experienced in my younger days, like when my biological dad died. I was nine years old, and my mom said to me, "Your father is in the hospital, Tharisse, and he may not make it. He had a bad drug reaction." I didn't even know what that meant at the time, but later found out he was a substance user and had gotten a hold of a bad batch of heroin. Naturally, I was devastated. Although my daddy didn't raise me full-time, I still knew him. I loved him. I recalled him loving me.

Experiencing loss by way of death is a feeling almost indescribable with words, especially for a young child. It can be quite confusing to an even younger one. I understood what my mother said to me when it happened, but I struggled with the *why* it had to happen.

I was getting ready for school one morning in early September; the school term had just begun. "He's gone, Tharisse. Your father passed away this morning," my mother relayed to me. She kept me home that day.

When I saw my daddy in his casket, it was an image never to be forgotten. Some years following his death, I lost my maternal grandmother; I called her Ma. I was co-raised by her and my mother. I had a very loving relationship with her. When she died, it made me feel so bad that I refused to attend her homegoing services. I couldn't let her go. It was like I was losing my loved ones quicker than I could handle. I lost both sets of my grandparents in a short period of time. My early teen years were filled with unfortunate circumstances. Grandma, Granddad, Ma, Daddy; I missed saying those words. I missed those people.

My feelings toward those losses were something else I kept to myself. Loss can cause a deep pulsating ache that nags away at you. It's typically called grief; it can last an uncertain amount of time and have effects on your life you may not be aware of.

The question the therapists tried to help me answer was: where do you look to seek comfort? They would say, "Tharisse, you can get through tough times; it's all about finding ways to cope." I tried, but I guess my ways of coping ended up working against me instead of for me.

The trauma caused by loss can definitely trigger depression, they would say, and I think that's how my illness began to creep its way out. I had issues with losing people I loved. A dark place was created, but I had no idea it would become my mind's regular hangout spot.

Sometimes, when I was depressed and laid in bed, I had racing thoughts. I tried to figure out how I got that way. Those thoughts made their way to my journal.

Dear Diary,

They say your body is your temple and it should be treated as such. Well, I didn't think much of my body, in fact, I hated it. I always wondered how most of the females in my family had nice shapely figures, smooth skin, both dark and light, just an overall feminine appearance. Whenever I looked in the mirror, I hated what I saw from head to toe; there were times I avoided mirrors entirely. I know you are supposed to love yourself and the body God has given you, but I just didn't. I wanted to be pretty. I wanted to have a

89

nice ass and wear jeans that hugged it perfectly. I wanted smooth skin. Shit! I wanted to feel sexy! I hated my acne, my hair, and my curveless body. I never felt sexy, ever! I would often avoid going places with my cousins because they were all pretty and shit; it made me feel like the ugly duckling. I think I have always had this issue. Even in my younger days hanging in the hood with my crew, I kind of felt like the ugly duckling of the bunch. Maybe that's why sex became an outlet for those hidden feelings and thoughts of myself. I didn't appreciate my body, so I easily gave it away to anyone who would have at it. I should have treated my body like a temple, respected it and took care of it. I wonder what people saw when they looked at me. Please, let people see me as beautiful. I want to be beautiful.

I had to learn to love myself and continued working toward that. Bipolar in its general meaning is having or relating to two poles or extremities. I often felt like I was living two separate lives as two different people.

Raising my daughter, it was important to me that she saw herself in a positive light. She was beautiful in the eyes of others, but she had to believe it within herself.

I would always put her in front of the mirror and say, "Destiny, look at yourself. Aren't you beautiful?" She had to learn to respect herself and her body. I encouraged her to believe she was good enough. It was my job. I had to teach her to respect other people's property and feelings; she needed to know and grow to treat others as she wanted to be treated.

This was a big part of the internal struggle. On the one hand, I had negative feelings about myself. Alternatively, I tried hard to prevent my Destiny from developing such feelings about herself. It was crazy living this double life. *Was I crazy?*

I cried a lot, wishing I didn't feel this way about myself. All I wanted was to be like others whom I admired, like friends whom I'd met that seemed so sure of themselves. Or, my beautiful cousins who didn't seem to question their beauty. I had received job training from leaders who were so smart and at the top of their professional game. I wanted to be like them, but I supposed I was mentally unhealthy.

Unfortunately, Destiny became a witness to the turmoil taking place within me.

CHAPTER SIX
HE LOVES ME, HE LOVES ME NOT
SHE LOVES ME, SHE LOVES ME NOT

2011 was the year. I had been with Dre for 'bout six years. We met when Destiny was around seven-years-old. He and I began as coworkers and friends, but it didn't remain that way for long. As Dre and I got to know each other outside of work, we both realized we were looking for the same thing in a relationship, which was loyalty. He led me to believe devotion was something that meant everything to him. I thought it would be perfect. I was willing to be faithful to anyone who was willing to actually be with me.

"Really, Dre, this is the real you, huh?" I asked him as his behavior became somewhat of a nuisance. "And, it took you three years to show da' fuck up," I sarcastically stated.

He bossed me around and questioned my every move. He even tried to school me on my daughter. No way was I having that. It was one thing that was made clear at the start of every relationship I'd been in after Eugene, and that was that no one would be replacing him, standing in for him, or any such thing. Destiny had lost her dad, and that was it. Was I wrong for that? Maybe, but Dre definitely had his hands full with his other children and was in no position to be giving parental advice to anyone else.

"Damn, this girl is so smart, Tharisse," he'd often say.

Their relationship started out okay, but she watched us like a hawk. She felt some type of way, but my involvement with Dre overshadowed mine with her.

"Woman, you betta get in that kitchen and whip something up," and "What took you so long to get home?" were things I heard from him often. I thought Dre meant well. For me, those were typical male demands. He had been badly scorned in his past relationship. He thought I was a good catch and undoubtedly didn't want to lose me. Initially, it was mild and easygoing. I had to be fair-minded to him. It was the *noble* thing to do, right?

It was at the beginning of our relationship when I decided to try to own my demon. We were on a date night, and we were sitting in a booth at The Diner on Springfield Ave. in Maplewood. "I have something to tell you, and I am not sure how this will affect us moving forward."

He looked at me expectantly. "Oh, gosh, what happened, Tharisse?"

I looked him in his big brown eyes, took a deep breath, and with a major case of the jitters, I said it. "I'm HIV positive."

The expression on his face scared me. That look of fear jumped out and choked me. His body erect. And, his nostrils flared. It seemed as if he was ready to get up and walk away.

"Whoa, girl, how can you just sit there and say that with a straight face? No, really, what's up, girl?" He glanced around the diner as if to be sure no one else could hear what we were talking about.

"I wouldn't play around with something like this. Trust me, I wish like hell I didn't have to say it at all, but I do. I need to say it because it's true, Dre." I explained the story to him. "I was nineteen years old when I found out. I wasn't a needle drug user or screwing around recklessly unprotected or anything of the sort. I simply fell in love and got caught out there."

I told Dre everything. He just sat there with his hands over his face. I couldn't tell if he was avoiding looking at me or if he was avoiding being seen. I didn't mean to insinuate that anyone who was an IV drug user deserved to get HIV, but it was all I could come up with at the time.

It wasn't until that moment that I learned that this illness did not discriminate. I definitely started that conversation all wrong. Dre had mentioned to me on another occasion that his sister battled with drug addiction, so not only did I say something stupid like that, but I just told this man I was infected with the virus. I had my fingers crossed underneath the table. Dre removed his hands from his face and revealed himself to me. He sat there and looked at me for a good ten minutes, not saying a single word. I watched tears fill those big brown eyes. His skin was caramel, and his hair was full of ocean-like waves. His shoulders were broad, and he had a slightly muscular build to him. I felt like shit for causing that tall, handsome guy to well up like that.

"Now what?" he said.

I removed my tightly crossed fingers and raised my hands from under the table. I reached out to hold his hands and waited.

He then grabbed hold of my hands and repeated, "Now what?"

When I heard the repeat of what I thought I heard, my eyes filled with tears as I interpreted it as us moving on together, but I needed to know for sure. I didn't want to make the mistake of making an ass out of myself by assuming. I took a moment before responding. I sat there and contemplated my situation for a moment.

Does this mean we may have a chance at moving forward? Could it be we just order our food, and this will be our last date night? Am I really being blessed with a decent man who can love me with my demon?

I sighed heavily.

If he decides to leave me at this point, I'm so done with trying to form relationships.

These were things circulating in my unhealthy mind.

We never did get to order our meals. Dre took me by the hand. "Come on, let me show you what I mean."

At his house that night, Dre made love to me in a way I had never experienced before. It was a blend of wearing my ass out yet allowing the tender moments to have a strong meaning. He was loving me. He gave me so much hope. We were together.

Our relationship taught me that despite all the stories I had ever read about people with HIV choosing not to disclose it to their sexual partners, it is possible that the person may still choose you. I knew Dre would have lots of questions, and he did, but just like me, he preferred to bury the thought, so we hardly talked about it. He made it clear how careful we would have to be, and I agreed.

Dre and I spent years loving one another, creating beautiful memories and getting to know each other on different levels until he eventually began showing his true colors with that controlling behavior. It had to have been there all along. Once it came to the surface, it reminded me of how much I hated the way Cliff spoke to my mother at times. I was not having that shit.

As my relationship with Dre went through a transition phase, I avoided him as much as possible. I started hanging out more often with my street sister, Tyson, from back in the day. As adults, over the years, we became the best of friends. Tyson was the only one that I had exposed my secret to from my old crew. She didn't judge or reject me. She chose to still see me as just Tharisse aka T-Money.

One Saturday night, we were sipping on some Verdi at her house. I said to Tyson, "We should go to NYC to chill for a while and get out of our comfort zone. We always sitting up in your crib, getting wasted. Let's get out of here before Dre does his usual pop up at your door act."

Tyson said to me, "Tharisse, what are you up to? I thought you said you weren't going out in public places anymore." She began to laugh as she continued to say, "You know he always showing up and embarrassing you."

I snickered. "Whatever! That shit ain't cool. Girl, he is really gettin' on my nerves. I'm not even sure if I still want him." I wasn't up to anything. I just felt like partying. Dre was always on my case about something, and I wanted to do something a little different in an unfamiliar atmosphere.

Tyson went along with it as she agreed that Dre was becoming a jerk. We knew he was a nice guy overall, but his ways were sickening.

Tyson and I went to this little spot in Brooklyn. We were dressed casually: jeans and tightly fitted tops. Tyson wore heels, but my tall ass didn't do the heel thing. I wore a low wedge instead. We were comfortable.

The music was poppin', and the flickering multi-colored lights hyped me up. I sat at the bar and ordered a margarita. In a matter of minutes, a girl bumped into me by accident. I could see she had way too many drinks in her system, so I just shrugged it off. Then, I felt someone come close to my ear and say, "Oh, my bad."

I slightly adjusted my body and replied, "It's cool, no biggie." She made a gesture as if she couldn't hear me because the music was so loud, so I came in close to her ear and repeated, "It's cool, no biggie." The girl smelled so good that I stayed up on her like a dog sniffing another dog's ass. "Oh, my goodness," I said to myself.

Tyson must have noticed me inhaling this woman because I felt her tapping the side of my leg.

"Tharisse, what are you doing?" Tyson quietly asked in my ear.

I backed my body away from the woman, but I wanted to know more about her. I was hypnotized by her scent just that quick.

"Yo', this chick over here smells sooooo good," I said to Tyson.

"I could tell by the way you were sniffing her. Why are you all up on that girl like that, T? You don't know her like that," Tyson replied.

I wasn't trying to hear what Tyson was talking. I leaned back over to the other side where the magic scent was and asked her if I could buy her a drink. She was beyond her limit, but that was typically how you expressed interest in someone at a bar. I had hoped not to sound cheesy, but she followed suit. Her smile was inviting.

"Yea, you can do that."

This was exactly what I needed—the different I was looking for.

Tyson already knew I had an attraction to females, although she never took it seriously when I talked about how good a girl's backside looked in some tight jeans or expressed how beautiful another girl looked in stretch pants.

That night, she got to see just how serious I was. I sat there with that beautiful stranger and chatted away as if I had just stumbled upon a new best friend.

Tyson allowed maybe thirty minutes or so to go by and then hit me with the okey-doke. "Tharisse, it's time we be heading out now."

I did not want to leave Shelly. I introduced them, "Tyson, this is Shelly, and Shelly, this is my best friend, Tyson."

Shelly said in a dry sort of way, "Sup."

Tyson said, "Hello," in a friendly tone.

Tyson gave me a grumpy look. It was time for me to leave Ms. Smell Good. Shelly and I exchanged numbers and said goodbye. Tyson and I left.

The next day, Tyson called me and asked, "What the hell was that about last night? You hitting on chicks now?"

I laughed. "Maybe."

Tyson replied, "Don't get stupid, Tharisse. You know Dre ain't trying to hear no shit like that."

I said, "Girl, her scent was like heaven; it opened me wide up."

"You crazy for real."

"Yea, I know."

After a short, mutual laugh, we hung up.

Of course, Dre grilled me about coming in the house so close to the break of dawn. "What kind of mother just hangs out all night at bars?" He went on and on. His manly chest was inflated. He was pounding his left fist into the palm of his right hand. "I'm not bouta have my lady ripping and running the streets all the time. Have some respect, Tharisse... for me and your daughter." My man was going off on me. He was trying to make me feel like I was doing something wrong just because I wanted to be free.

"Dre, mothers go out and party sometimes, and it's not a crime. Loosen the hell up!" I debated.

I knew my feelings towards Dre were changing. We were still cool, but I wasn't really attracted to him anymore. I didn't know what was happening. I carried on as I pleased. He was making it easy for me to break our commitment to one another. Besides, Destiny didn't like Dre all that much anyway. She was used to having all my attention. There was lots of bickering between to the two of them. I always reminded Des to respect her elders, but Dre was as childish as he could be. I told him he was skating on thin ice.

"I'm not gonna be held captive in this relationship, Dre," I boldly said.

"What?" he shouted.

"Yea, this ain't the Stone Age." I shook my head with contempt, but I continued a relationship with him anyhow.

It wasn't like I didn't care about how Destiny felt about him or our relationship. It's just I chose to ignore my daughter's feelings. The unrecognizable me had emerged. One minute, I felt sane and within reason, the next I was uncontrollable. I thought, as the mother, it was my choice to make and not my daughter's. Yup, I was starting to place my Destiny in an unhealthy home environment. Who had I become?

A few days went by, and I still hadn't heard from Shelly. No call, no text. I was waiting patiently, but it was wearing thin. All I could think about was how she smelled. Plus, her body was tight and just right. I remembered asking her what she had on that night, and she told me it was Dolce & Gabbana Light Blue™. It became my new fave. Shelly probably didn't realize it, but she had hooked me.

Late Wednesday night, Dre and I were in bed, indulging in a little foreplay. As I uninterestedly performed my womanly duties on him, I heard my phone chime. I stopped and reached for it.

"Oh, hell no, what the fuck are you doing, girl?" Dre yelled as he was just about to climax.

I didn't care. I was eager to see if it was Shelly. I looked at my phone, and it was a text from her: *Whaddup, it was nice talking with you the other night. I know I was tore up. Is this a bad time? How are you?*

According to Dre, it was a terrible time. "I know damn well you not on your phone," he unhappily said.

I probably should have at least finished him off, but I didn't. His nuts left abandoned. Sweat danced angrily upon his forehead. He jumped out of bed, and his dick went to swinging and swaying.

"Man, are you crazy?" I asked. "You should see yourself right now. Put that thing away."

"You put it away. You da' crazy one here. You don't just stop sucking a man's dick mid-suck!"

That moment was another indicator that something different was happening. My actions following that moment began to show disrespect towards my relationship with Dre.

Shelly and I were texting each other all the time. It progressed to phone calls. During one late-night phone conversation held while I was soaking in a warm bath, she asked me something, and I wasn't sure how I should have responded.

"Tharisse, so, are you gay? Lesbian, I mean," she asked with a sense of confidence.

My body's position changed from laying back to sitting straight up in the water. I didn't want to blow my chances with her.

"Not exactly. I've been with females before, but I don't label myself as lesbian or bisexual," I hesitantly said because it was the actual truth. I didn't want her to think I was a newbie to that lifestyle.

"Sooo... you have a boyfriend then?"

"Hold on a sec. Let me get out this tub. You bouta have me in here drowning 'n shit." I absolutely did not want to admit to Shelly that I, in fact, had a boyfriend, but just when I was about to lie to her, in walked Dre. He had come into the bathroom and caught me with my phone in hand.

"Woman, have you lost your damn mind? Who are you talking to this time of night? It better be your mother!" Dre made sure he was heard by the person on the other end of my line.

I couldn't lie at this point. She heard him.

"Who is that, Tharisse? Your boyfriend?"

I was pissed at Dre. Pretending it wasn't a big deal, I said, "Please hold on, Shelly."

Dre demanded an answer from me. "Who the hell is Shelly?" His nostrils flared again.

I put my phone on mute. I was so fuckin annoyed with him.

"She is a friend I just met. Dre, why are you acting like this?" I tried to be unflustered.

We were arguing at a volume that could have easily been considered alarming, given the time of night it was. I awkwardly got back to my call with Shelly and asked if I could call her tomorrow.

She calmly said, "Aight yo'."

I worried she was done after hearing Dre. I told him he was overreacting, and he should chill out. We were shacking up, but it was my apartment, and Dre knew I could have him leave at any moment. It didn't stop him from getting bent out of shape because of my actions. He had a look in his eyes I didn't like. It made me nervous. He never raised his hand to me, but the glare on his face and the way his fists were clenched sure made it seem as if he was close. I went and slept in the living room.

I continued to get to know Shelly, and we were in our own kind of relationship. I managed to convince her that Dre and I were no longer exclusive. She wasn't down for a triangle love affair, and neither was I. We never did the ménage à trois thing, but my movements became outlandish and out of control. I had lured her into my distorted web of a life.

I forced Dre to sleep on the bedroom floor; it allowed Shelly to sleep in the bed with me. She and I made love and didn't care about him getting any sleep. Sometimes, I even made him sleep outside in the car.

Dre resulted to constantly reminding me of how he chose to be with me regardless of my HIV status. "You got a lot of nerve after all we been through, Tharisse. You being real stupid. I hope she worth it."

I suppose I should have been grateful to Dre given the fact that he stuck around. I didn't realize at the time Dre had become my ride or die despite the many flaws within our relationship. I hadn't quite gained an understanding of what I was doing to him or how selfish I must've seemed.

Our arguing extended beyond our home environment and into our workplace. I was blurting out stuff without thinking first, and so was he. I began to disrespect him in front of others. He was infuriated. I was indignant.

We never took a moment to acknowledge the fact that we also had an impressionable young teen at home witnessing all the disturbing behavior taking place around her. I was Des's mother, and I was crazed out of my mind. I no longer cared about anyone's feelings other than my own. I became unintentionally inconsiderate.

Clearly, I should have stayed on my meds or at least involved therapy in some type of way. I was what they called manic. Being bipolar had infiltrated my being. I wasn't aware of the damage I was doing. I was reckless, careless, and downright destructive.

As my downward spiral continued, Dre and I decided it was time to attempt a civil conversation. Destiny stayed at my parents' house for a couple of nights. It was perfect timing to try to lay some shit out. While the E&J we drank was probably not a good idea, things were going well. I apologized for most of my actions, and he reciprocated. It had been a long time since Dre had a piece of me; I caved to his horny advances.

We were knocking the headboard fairly hard. We were romantically reconnecting and heard nothing but each other's moans of passion. We did not hear Shelly open the bedroom door. I had given her keys with the agreement that she would call or text first before just showing up. That day, of all days, she decided not to oblige.

"Wow, T! Really?" she said disappointedly.

Dre was eager to respond to her seeing us like that. He constrained me with his weight, which prevented me from getting up. Dre took complete advantage to have a moment of revenge. "Now, bitch, how you feel?"

I screamed hysterically, "Dre, get the fuck off me!"

I saw how disgusted Shelly was with me. She appeared grossed out as she watched him get his naked ass up from the bed. Dre began to dress, and I couldn't take my eyes off her. I feared the Bronx in her was ready to kick my ass. I slowly stood up in total disgrace.

"I am so sorry, Shelly," I pleaded. "I am so sorry for all of this."

Dre looked at her with evil in his eyes. I couldn't imagine Dre putting his hands on Shelly. He wasn't violent, but I knew oh so well how emotional distress could lead you places you never thought you'd go. I was terrified of what could possibly happen. Dre didn't hit Shelly; his next move was far worse. I never thought I would hear the words that came out of his mouth. The liquor made him momentarily insane, or he was amped up because of the piece of ass he had just pulled out of.

"Did she tell you she was sick while you were so busy falling in love with her?"

I turned into the exorcist. My head swiftly turned to Dre. Panicked, I hovered my hand over his mouth and yelled, "Dre, shut the fuck up! Don't you dare say another word! You are crossing the fuckin' line, and I'm telling you NOT. ANOTHER. GOT. DAMN. WORD!" My heart was pounding. My head was spinning. I suddenly felt emotionally nauseous.

Shelly sat herself down on the ottoman in the corner of my bedroom. She asked me in a shallow, confused voice,

"T, what is he talking about? Did he say sick? Like, sick how?"

Although she practically whispered, she sounded so loud. Shelly began blurting all kinds of questions, one after another. She didn't give me time to answer.

I was shaking and felt my stomach churning. I owed her the truth. In my head, I heard my own voice pushing me to tell her. *Say it. Say it.*

"Baby, he is talking about HIV." Repeatedly, I said, "I am so sorry. Please, I am so damn sorry."

The hurt covered her face. "Tharisse, you bitch! You made me fall in love with you knowing you were with this dude, and now this?"

I crumbled to pieces inside.

Dre lit a cigarette; he stood there nodding his head with a slight grin. The room flooded with Shelly's tears, my tears. This was a mess I created. I felt drowned. Submerged in a sea of my own sorrow. I was so in love with her. To have inflicted this amount of pain on her filled me with remorse. *Who am I? What have I done?*

Shelly made me feel like the woman I yearned to be. She thought I was pretty. She told me I was sexy. Even though my mind was obviously not well, I owed my femininity to her. How could I let my status get revealed to her like that? It should have come from my lips; words I

110

was too afraid to say to her. I don't think Shelly knew how much of a hold she had on me.

All of a sudden, the speed of the earth had slowed down enough for me to realize for sure that I didn't know who I was anymore. The two of them were as special to me as I had ever known special to be. Overall, Dre was a decent guy who worked so hard to please me and chose to love me. Shelly was this sexy ass chick straight outta the Bronx with an attitude that somehow turned me on, but she was also a gentle soul. I had damaged them both. I manipulated their hearts and destroyed their acts of love.

I reached out to hug Shelly and asked her if she was okay, although I knew she couldn't possibly be.

"Don't fuckin' touch me, Tharisse. Don't you ever fuckin' touch me again!" Her words were bubbling with hatred as she stormed out of the room and left. As soon as she was gone, I told Dre to get the fuck out.

I was in a crisis, a state of emergency. There was one person I needed to hear from right then, and that was my godmother, Cora. I could only hope her godly words would be enough to help me see some light. My world got darker by the minute. I called her on the phone. She didn't answer, but I anticipated she'd tell me to pray.

I needed help holding on. I should have been praying for some strength; instead, I fell to my knees and prayed for Shelly.

"Please make sure she is alright. Please, Lord, don't make her sick. All she did was fall in love. I am already suffering through this. Please punish me, not her. I know I messed up. Please!" I belted out to the heavens, "PLEEEEASE!"

CHAPTER SEVEN
MY DARKEST MOMENT

During my darkest moments, I envied the dead. In my twisted mind, I thought they were fortunate to not be here on Earth anymore to go through all the bullshit we go through. I was jealous that they were someplace in peace, and I wasn't. That negative perception had me screwed up. I had planned to maximize the time I was blessed with and hoped to find and fulfill the very purpose of my life. I failed.

My broken wings were on their way to being healed and restored. I should've been stronger. I thought I had grown spiritually enough to conquer anything that came my way. I found comfort in believing God made no mistakes and that He doesn't give us more than we could bear. This was heavy, though. I was let down again by what life had given me. It was time for me to take responsibility for the pain I'd caused others. I had come to the end of the road. It was time for me to let go of everything and everyone.

Dear Diary,

Drowning in my sorrows, I listened to Boyz II Men's rendition of "It's So Hard to Say Goodbye to Yesterday" while writing my goodbye letters to my parents and only child. The pain I felt from that day of events with Dre, Shelly and I was more than I could bear. God had to know that. The darkness from it all was blinding. Leaving these goodbyes weren't as hard to say as the song indicated.

To my mother (Jackie),

If you are reading this, it's probably because I am no longer around. I know you are most likely sickened with grief, but I just want you to know how much I truly loved you. Mommy, I love you so much that I am asking for your forgiveness. Please forgive me for not seeing you for who and what you truly are. My mind was in such a negative place that it hindered me from seeing any of the beauty in the world. I saw you as selfish, when in fact, you are the most selfless person I know. I saw you as weak, and you are quite the opposite of that. You are incredibly strong. I doubted your love for me. Through our growing relationship, I can now see just how much you loved me. These things have been shown to me by the force

114

of God; He has made his light shine within you and that, in turn, caused me to take a second look at you. It was that very same light that encouraged me to take a second look at myself as well. I want you to know, Mommy, that I do not blame you for my life and the sickness in it. No one is at fault for such unforeseeable devastation, not even the one that has led you to this letter. Do not blame yourself for my choices as I have learned to accept you for yours. I ask that you make God the leader in your life as He will be the one to see you through. I love you from heaven where I shall rest until we meet again.

Forever love,

Tharisse, your first-born daughter

To Cliff (my stepfather),

Thank you for being you. I appreciate all your efforts. Getting to know you over the years as the father figure in my life has helped me in so many ways. It's because of you and your relationship with my mother that I always second guess my relationships. It made me vow to never depend on another to shelter, feed or gift me. I was caught up loving a man because he was willing to take care of me by providing materialistic things I thought were important. That concept died with him.

115

It is the things deemed priceless that hold so much more meaning and substance than what money can buy. I did not allow that to capture me ever again, and furthermore, it taught me to teach my own daughter the importance of working hard for whatever it is she may want in life. I also taught her to be open to love and compromise in her relationships. Thank you for the good lessons I learned just because you were you. I am not angry, bitter, nor am I ashamed of these feelings. It is my hope that you aren't either.
Love, Tharisse

My Dearest Destiny,
Baby girl, you already know! I have spent your entire life expressing my love for you. I know at times you may have questioned it, but deep in your heart, you always knew. I first want you to try to understand that my exit from your life is in no way your fault, nor is it mine. Mommy was dealing with issues that simply got the best of her. You are the best thing that ever happened to me, hence your name. You were my Destiny. Please believe me when I say that I tried really hard to give you a fulfilling life as your mother. Can you find it in your heart to forgive me? I beg this of you. Despite my struggles, I take pride in the mother

you brought out of me, but I am ashamed of the mother I allowed my illnesses to turn me into. It is my prayer that you are able to forgive me and move past it. I allowed my unhealthy mind to take control of my life, but you can claim victory over yours. Destiny, my sweet daughter, you are in good health. God has given me the ultimate gift, which was for you to be born without any sicknesses, and to Him, I am forever grateful. You were the air that sustained me. You were my reason to carry on, thus far. You were the triumph in me. I made a choice, Destiny, and it had nothing to do with you. It was a point I had come to in my life when I felt beyond repair. I taught you that life is about choices and decisions and that we should own them. I will own mine, so you don't have to. Let your heart be free from any shame, guilt or negativity as a result of my choices. I ask that you keep God first, Destiny; lean on Him. Chase your dreams, all those things you always said you wanted to do. College awaits you. The big screen awaits you. Love, family, and success await you. Do your thang, Des, and when it's your God-willed time to join me in heaven, Mommy and Daddy will await you.

Destiny Maliah Washington, you are worthy!
I love you and then some!

Mommy

Lord, as I make my way... allow my heart to lead me to my happiness. I release all the built-up negativity in order to make room for something positive. I am weak, Lord. Please forgive me for my sins, I repented. I wanted to be welcomed into the gates of Heaven. I left my journal back in the house in plain sight, sure to be found.

It was a crisp and clear day out. I was driving in my midnight blue 2001 BMW 528i up I-78, heading towards NYC, Destiny riding shotgun. I wanted to die in NYC to make a statement. I wanted Shelly to know I took my last breath on her turf, knowing what I had done to her. I blasted the volume, playing all my favorite old school jams like "Love Sensation" by Loleatta Holloway, "Love Injection" by Trussell, "Still in Love" by Meli'sa Morgan and Stevie Wonder's "All I Do," just to name a few.

Frantically taking the sleeping pills I had tucked away in my medicine cabinet, I explained to Destiny how I could no longer fight what seemed to be a losing battle. The pain felt from heartbreak ran so deep in me, it took me to a place I never thought I'd go. I lowered the volume of my music.

My daughter had no business in that car with me, but I needed to tell her why I would no longer be with her. My sweet, innocent child needed to know that she was not to blame for any of the madness her mommy created in their lives.

"Listen to me, baby, you know Mommy loves you, right?" I said to her. "Mommy can't live like this anymore; I have to let you go. You can live without me, baby, and be just fine... probably even better."

Destiny was trembling in fear as she belted out, "Mommy, stop! You scaring me. I don't wanna—"

I interrupted her, "Stop, Des, listen to me. I can't, alright? I need to tell you something first, baby. You know I love you, but I lied before, Des. I lied about how your daddy died."

The pills I'd been popping while I drove began to take effect. I continued to traumatize my young daughter and told her, "Ya' father didn't die from no heart attack. He died because he was sick with AIDS! Des... he was sick, baby, and he left me with it! He made Mommy sick!"

As the car swerved, I knew it was time to get Destiny out before I did something even more regrettable. I didn't want to take my daughter to the gates of Heaven with me. She had a life to live.

I continued to explain. "You're okay, though, Destiny. You hear me? You're okay, baby. I'm just tired of hurting,

Des. Mommy can't do it anymore; it's too hard being like this."

I told her to take my cell phone and call her grandma to come get her. I no longer had any resentment towards Jackie; I had learned to forgive her. I prayed she would care for her granddaughter in such a way that superseded her care for me.

I slowed the car down along the shoulder to let Destiny out. Then, I slowly pulled off. "Oh God, please forgive me. I love my Destiny so much... probably too much. Please, Lord, take care of my baby girl," I prayed aloud.

Despite my slipping away into unconsciousness, I could hear in the far distance a cry out from Destiny.

"Mommyyyyy! Mommyyyyy!"

CHAPTER EIGHT

WAKE UP!

"*Please, I need you to wake up. Open your eyes for me. I need you. I love you. I see how hard you tried to fight, but I wanna help you now. I am so mad at you for trying to leave me. How could you leave me when you said you loved me? Please just wake up,*" I heard a voice say.

I woke up in a hospital. I didn't know where I was or how I got there. I felt like I had been beaten on; I was so stiff. My mouth was dry, and my throat was blocked. I tried to speak but couldn't.

As I looked around to gain focus, I saw my daughter. I slowly reached out to her. It must have been her voice I heard. I could tell by the expression on her face that she was not only disappointed in me, but she also appeared angry. I understood why. I remembered what I had done. I traumatized my daughter.

Shit!

I was disappointed to be alive. I looked to the other side of the room and was shocked to see Dre and Shelly sitting in the corner. *Oh no! What in the hell are they doing here? How did they know? Who called them?* I wondered. They both must have still loved me enough to be there. Both of them sat in silence with their faces lit with a sense of happiness as they saw me reach for Des. I supposed they were relieved I had awakened. *It's funny how God will force you to face the very things you are quick to run away from.*

As the three loves of my life came to my bedside and stood there watching over me, I could feel the love that filled that hospital room.

I had a decision to make. As much as I loved Dre and Shelly, I loved my Destiny more than I could ever say. Even though my actions probably showed differently, I needed to prove to her just how much she meant to me. There was work I needed to do to repair what I had destroyed.

A doctor came in the room and said, "It's nice to see you awake, Ms. Washington. We are going to remove the breathing tube now. I need you to try to remain calm."

I was still confused.

He continued, "You have been asleep for quite some time. Do you remember anything about what caused your accident?"

As I choked, gasping to take that first breath, I acted as if I didn't know what he was talking about. I just wanted out of there. I whispered, "No, Doc, I don't."

He then went on to explain. "Well, fortunately, you sustained only minor bodily harm from the crash. We need to run some further testing now that you have awakened from the coma."

I interrupted in a raspy voice. "Wait, what coma? How long have I been here like this, and where is my mother?"

My thirteen-year-old daughter lightly admonished me, "Ma, calm down! You been asleep for about a week. Grandma is here, and yes, I called them here too. I knew that even with whatever twisted love affair you had going on, you would want them to know if you died or not. They could have said no, but hey, look around, here they are."

Dre and Shelly just sat there quietly. From their silence, I could tell they had nothing to say at that moment. I looked at Shelly, and she seemed like she wanted to cry, but I didn't know if it was sadness or anger on her face.

Then, the doctor shooed them all out. "Okay, I need you all to clear the room for a while. I need to examine my patient and continue bringing her up to speed."

I asked Destiny to call her grandmother so that she could help me understand all the doctor was saying. My mother had probably already spoken with the doctors about my condition. She was most likely mad as hell. Our relationship was nothing less than complicated, but I was her firstborn. That had to count for something.

Destiny replied, attitude thick in her voice, "Yes, Ma, I will go get her now."

While I waited for my mom to come, the doctor stepped out after examining me. I delicately called out to Shelly. She came right in.

"Babe, let me explain, please," I begged her.

She stopped me and said, "Tharisse, you have a lot going on. I'm not sure what point you were trying to make, but they said you took a bunch of painkillers while driving. Were you trying to kill yourself?"

I didn't want to lie to this girl anymore; I was just thankful she was there.

"Yea, Shelly. I know it was stupid. I was a coward. I didn't want to face the mess I had made. I disappointed you. I am ashamed. I love you so much. I apologize, Shelly. Can you ever forgive me?" I choked and couldn't stop coughing, but I had so much to say.

Shelly handed me a cup of water as she answered, "Because I am a woman of God, I have already forgiven you, T." She went on before I could get my hopes up. "And, while I still love you, I just can't be with you." She shook her head. "T, you broke our trust, but you didn't break me."

Honestly, I wasn't expecting Shelly to stay in a relationship with me after all I had put her through. She was strong. She didn't let me break her. She just had to be okay. I admired her strength throughout our time together. Her touch always stayed with me. Her scent I never forgot. Before she left, Shelly turned to look at me and gave me one final bit of wisdom.

"Tharisse, I'm glad you woke up. I pray you deal with your inner issues so that you can focus on your other health problems. I will be getting tested soon. I'm scared and worried that you may have gotten me sick, but I got my faith and hope that I am okay. I have a life, and my family will be devastated if some shit like that happened to me. You know how they all count on me. Tharisse, I gotta go. Bye."

"Please, just let me know how your test goes," I shamefully said to her. It was my final words to Shelly just before she walked out of the room and my life forever. She didn't respond; she just left.

Dre came right in as Shelly walked out.

I asked him, "Why you here, Dre? After everything, why are you here?"

He raised an eyebrow and replied, "Oh, so you do remember everything? You lied to the doctor when he asked you what led you here. You still lying."

I huffed and said, "Okay, so I lied. This is too much to deal with, Dre. It's just too much." I began to cry, and Dre came closer to me and grabbed hold of my hand.

He said, "Yea, I know it is. That's why I'm here. We didn't know how this was gonna go. Your little girlfriend was scared shitless. Damn, she loved you, Tharisse. I told her I was sorry for saying what I said to her. It wasn't my place. She told me to kick rocks. I took it like a man, though. I was wrong."

I stopped him from saying any more, and just as I was about to respond, my mother and Destiny walked in the room. I dragged my eyes away from my mother and glanced at Dre. "You should go."

He simply nodded and left.

My mother came over to the bed and started right in on me. "Okay, now what the hell, Tharisse? You scared the hell out of all of us. Your brother and sister are so confused. You need to talk to them. They are worried about you."

"And, what about you?" I asked.

"What about me? I'm good. I know you a fool, but I also know you ain't going nowhere no time soon. Don't try this shit no more, Tharisse. How you feel now?" she asked.

"I'm okay," I assured her.

I was still sore all over, but I could feel the drugs soothing my system. I was more concerned with how everyone else was. I felt bad for surviving and so ashamed of everything. I could tell by my mother's behavior that we weren't going to talk about a suicide attempt any more than we spoke of my being diagnosed with HIV. Everyone has their own way of coping with difficult situations, and I suppose my mom had hers.

The doctor also told me I would be speaking with a psychiatrist later on that evening. I knew that order was coming. I watched Destiny as the docs were talking, and I saw how frightening it all was for her.

Once the doctors left, I asked Des if we could talk.

She said, "Ma, you just need to rest. I'm alright. I just want you to focus on getting better. Please, I need you."

At that moment, I wondered how my daughter had matured so much in a matter of a week. The truth was she had always been my rock. She was my destiny.

The choice I needed to make was staring me in the face. I chose her. I chose my daughter. I told her she was right; I needed to focus on my health.

"Des, I love you, baby. We will talk about all of this once I make it out of here. I will be fine." I said the words to her with pure intentions, but I was scared all over again. I didn't know if we could heal from such a terrible ordeal, an attempt to end my life.

My mother and Destiny left for the night and told me they would be back the next morning. I was alright with that. I needed some alone time to figure some shit out. I just lay there with all kinds of thoughts roaming my mind.

The psychiatrist finally came and spoke with me. I told him I made a mistake and that I wasn't trying to kill myself. I did not want them trying to commit me to a psych unit. I had to say whatever it took to clear myself so that my daughter didn't spend any more time without her mother. I figured if I wasn't successful in taking my own life, God had already forgiven me. I fell asleep praying for the strength to pick up the pieces.

The break of dawn crept in, and the sunrise peeked at me through the hospital blinds. I felt God's reassurance. Strength began to set in, and I was ready to go home. They released me four days later. I was put on a mild antidepressant medication, and they also started me on antiretrovirals for the HIV.

My mother insisted I come stay with them for a few days so she could look out for me. I didn't refuse the help.

She and Cliff made sure I had everything I needed to be comfortable.

I was beginning to gain a sense of hope again. It was almost like my mind did a reset. God definitely had a plan for my life. He made it clear to me that He would see me through it all. I didn't feel attacked anymore. I realized I wasn't being punished. The lies I told, the deceit, were all mistakes in judgment. All of a sudden, I wanted to move past the darkness. I wanted to live.

As I spent the next two weeks recuperating at my parents' house, I spoke with my brother and sister about everything that had been going on.

Junior asked, confusion written all over his face, "T, are you a lesbian now?"

I laughed for the first time in a while and told him no. I explained to them both that sometimes life and all of its ups and downs can confuse you.

"I know I haven't quite been myself for a while now, but I was sick in more than one way. I'm fine now though, and I want you guys to know I love you dearly. I am still your big sister, and I hope I haven't failed you."

Jasmine shocked me when she responded, "You haven't failed us, T. We love you. And, I didn't like that girl Shelly anyways. Is she gone now?"

I was thrown by hearing that from my little sister, but hey, she was growing up too and had formed her own opinions of things.

With a small smile, I nodded. "Yea, she is gone."

Having that conversation with Junior and Jasmine reassured me I was still being looked up to, despite my flaws. I never did tell them about the virus. They weren't ready to handle it. But then again, who was I to make that decision for them? Maybe Destiny wasn't ready to hear it, and I cheated her. I had many indiscretions to own up to. I was awakening.

I came to a huge decision. Once Destiny got out of high school and went off to college, I would make every effort possible to try something different. The thought of being alone was scary, but I felt it was necessary. It became my new goal. I only had a few years to plan things out and decide where my new life would be.

So, I said goodbye to relationships for the time being. I wanted to only focus on reconnecting with my daughter. I had a lot of work ahead of me health-wise, both mentally and emotionally. I continued to pray for the strength to carry on. I began to look forward to a new life once again in a new place all on my own. I started my journey to healthy living. I was ready to be better.

My mornings were no longer dreadful. I'd look for the smell of a fresh day as the visuals from my dreams faded to reality. I'd wake out my sleep grateful instead of hateful. I started a work-at-home data entry job shortly after leaving my parents' house.

"Hey, Ma, wanna do lunch?" I called and asked Jackie on my days off.

"Yeah, we could do lunch," she would answer me with excitement tucked lightly behind her words.

I made it a thing to get to know my mom again through my new lenses on life. She and I laughed our asses off during our what became weekly lunch meetings. She bought me the new iPhone© so that I could capture any special moment. I felt we were getting closer.

Despite all that had transpired and all that was to come, I enjoyed life. I got a high from thoughts of my future. I dreamed again about what life could be like. Where would I move to? Should I buy a new car? It was the mentioning of my inner thoughts to Destiny that gave her hope. She was happy and thriving. I prayed for her life to be as fulfilling as she saw fit. I prayed she escaped any turmoil I may have placed upon her.

Dre sent me a text saying he turned out fine. He couldn't say the words, but I knew he meant he went and got tested. It was negative. I told him I loved him and wished him well, but I never knew with Dre. That text may or may not have been the last I'd ever hear from him.

I never did hear anything else from Shelly. I imagined if she received bad news from her testing, she would have made it known. Knowing her the way I did, she had moved on with her life and was doing just fine. I continued to believe we were soulmates although we couldn't be together. Another broken heart.

As I take this moment to look back on my life, I saw how I was living to die, but then I decided to live. I was given a second chance to get it right.

SPECIAL MESSAGE
FROM THARISSE

DEMONS

I was invaded by a demon, an uninvited guest that announced its presence quite some time ago. Although I have managed to somehow learn to share myself with it, I still never understood why it chose my territory to invade. Apparently, this demon doesn't discriminate when deciding where to create its chaos. It doesn't matter who you are or where you're from. It plays this crazy game of roulette and fires its multiple shots randomly, and where they land is who gets wounded with the fatal disease. I was hit a few times, not even knowing I had to be on the lookout for such evil.

The demon made its way in me, and instead of occupying space in my body solely, it decided to have parties whenever it chose to and invited other unwelcomed guests to attend. They had themselves a good ole time in me. I would have never thought I'd be considered the company for this type of crowd, but when you are dealing

133

with bullies of this nature, one never knows why they are chosen.

I hate my demon and all its friends, not only because I didn't invite them in the first place, but because I had no choice in allowing them to become a part of me. The demon itself makes me feel some type of way; it makes me think some type of way. Sometimes, I still have a hard time figuring out who I truly am because it's been a part of me for so long. It has its own way of influencing you, one way or the other. I try all the time not to weaken. I look for ways to evict the demon from my dwelling; nothing seems to work. This demon is a stubborn son of a bitch and refuses to leave my property. I am constantly seeking counsel to join the battlegrounds against it, but there hasn't been anything intelligent enough, aggressive enough, brave enough, to join forces with me. I do, however, know of a powerful force that can blow this demon, along with its occasional party hoppers, right out of the water, but I guess in some way that force is with me. (Hence, I am here to share this with you.)

That almighty force is doing what it can. I have been able to show the demon I am not the one to be fucked with. You will not defeat me, no matter how big your parties are. No matter how often you and your guests try to make your existence known, I shall not surrender to you.

My demon is very loyal and makes it clear to me all the time that regardless of how much I turn my back on it or tell it that it's not welcomed, it's here for the long haul.

Despite its intention, I managed to contain the invasion. I really didn't know how my circle of family and friends would react to me letting them in on what was taking place within me. Would they think of me as some type of weirdo, or would they be understanding and non-judgmental, maybe even join the battle against my demon and its circle of family and friends?

Oh yes, you see my demon functions almost like you and me. The demon reproduces, which means little demons are running about, invading people too. It has cousins and in-laws and shit that go around seeking out the next area to start popping off randomly. It is a crazy family to deal with. They don't discriminate, and they get a fuckin' insane sense of enjoyment playing the twisted game of roulette. I had to find a way to go on with life with my demon and its crew.

Sometimes, I try to talk rationally with my demon and simply ask it to leave, telling it I don't appreciate being taken advantage of. And being the selfless person I am, I also ask on behalf of others that may have gotten caught in the crossfire. "Demon, why do you do this? Do you realize how much havoc you wreak on innocent lives?"

You see, demons are disguised; they come in all forms of life and circumstance. They are hidden within everything that serves us in this world. They lay dormant within people and money. Also, beware, love and relationships can lead you to the very place and time where the next random hit will be. Sometimes, demons are invited, but most of the time, they aren't. I certainly didn't invite mine, or did I send an invitation unintentionally? I often ask myself that question, but it's normal to question what you don't understand. Meanwhile, I am aware that I wasn't targeted, but it frustrates the hell out of me not knowing the WHY?

I didn't die upon invasion, at least not in the flesh, but being invaded by this demon murdered the part of my soul where it resides. It is locked there; it is behind that hidden door that leads to that dark place. It is where the demon held me captive for a while until I was able to break free and lock it away, hoping it will never get out. It is behind that door where all the action takes place when the demon decides to invite others in. The demon doesn't party as often as it once did, but I can tell when it is holding meetings with those within its circle of family and friends, strategizing against me.

This is my truth, and I know there are others who may feel as though they've been invaded by a demon. My message to you is, "Don't let the demon win. Fight that muthafucka with all your might. It and its family are cruel, yet you cannot let them defeat you."

I consider myself somewhat on the intelligent side. I am thinking about shaking things up a bit where that dark, hidden place lies within. I wonder what will happen if I open the door and let some natural light in that bitch and expose the demon, showing it that I am no longer afraid of it. The demon did always seem to prefer being in the dark, and that's why I think it drags me there. But no more! I am opening up the door...

I have decided to own my life with the demon, so here is my truth. Allow me to formally introduce myself. My name is Tharisse Washington, and I am HIV positive. Yes, it has been extremely difficult carrying the weight of it on my shoulders, but my demon has taught me tons of valuable lessons in life and continues to do so.

I look forward to a happy life with my daughter and her growth into womanhood. I'm sure our conversations will be interesting. Like her mama, she has a lot to show this world.

Self-awareness is key!
I never knew it existed, but there it was all along.

DEAR READER

If you are not familiar with the terms HIV and AIDS, I highly suggest you do some basic research as everyone living on this planet earth should have some type of awareness to this epidemic.

What Is HIV?

Basically, HIV stands for human immunodeficiency virus. It is the virus that can lead to acquired immunodeficiency syndrome, or AIDS, if not treated.

According to the USA CDC, in 2017, 38,739 people received an HIV diagnosis in the US. Although the annual number of new HIV diagnoses remained stable between 2012 and 2016, we still have so much more work to be done in our efforts towards ending the stigma that blanket the lives of those living with HIV and AIDS.

If these stats are not alarming enough, as we break down the total number of people receiving an HIV diagnosis, the age range that holds the highest among these diagnosed are between 25 years old and 34 years old.

Being an advocate for lives affected by HIV/AIDS, I tried to do my best to present a realistic account for a young life receiving such a difficult diagnosis, and I encourage others to get tested, know your status. There are people in the same predicament and willing to provide support. As a society, we must find a way to unite and encourage one another to live our best lives. We find a way to be receptive to open communication when it comes to chronic illness, both visible and invisible illnesses. One must ask themselves, how can I do my part in the prevention of the spread of HIV/AIDS even though I am not directly affected? I thank you for purchasing/reading Unbreak My Heart, and it is my sincerest hope that you join in the fight. If you know someone who has been diagnosed HIV positive and don't quite know how to be supportive, the best thing you can do is educate yourself on the topic. That's it. It is understood by many that this is a very personal issue in one's life and a conversation that is not so easy to discuss. Hence, another of my reasons why I chose to listen to God's calling on my life and share this story with you.

Here are a few resources to get you started on your research quest:

http://www.unaids.org/

https://www.aidsmap.com/resources

https://www.hiv.gov/

https://www.greaterthan.org/state-hiv-aids-hotlines/

https://www.apa.org/pi/aids/resources/index.aspx

*Google it and get educated.

~Kashinda